"It's time to say goodbye."

Once upon a time, Melody would have complied because she wasn't accustomed to having to beg or grovel or make scenes. But that was before James had ignited a passion in her that refused to be hindered either by pride or propriety. At the prospect of losing him, she broke loose with a raging madness she was helpless to control.

"You *are* my life, James!" she cried, and catapulted herself into his unwilling arms.

Catherine Spencer, once an English teacher, fell into writing through eavesdropping on a conversation about Harlequin Romance novels. Within two months she changed careers and sold her first book. She moved to Canada from England thirty years ago and lives in Vancouver. She is married to a Canadian and has four grown children—two daughters and two sons—plus three dogs and a cat. In her spare time she plays the piano, collects antiques and grows tropical shrubs. Catherine Spencer was a finalist in the Romance Writers of America (RITA) competition with *The Loving Touch*.

Books by Catherine Spencer

HARLEQUIN ROMANCE
3138—WINTER ROSES

LADY BE MINE
Catherine Spencer

Harlequin Books

TORONTO • NEW YORK • LONDON
AMSTERDAM • PARIS • SYDNEY • HAMBURG
STOCKHOLM • ATHENS • TOKYO • MILAN
MADRID • WARSAW • BUDAPEST • AUCKLAND

ISBN 0-373-03348-6

LADY BE MINE

Copyright © 1993 by Kathy Garner.

First North American Publication 1995.

Printed in U.S.A.

CHAPTER ONE

SHE must have fallen asleep with her head hanging over like a broken doll's because his voice, coming out of nowhere as it did, had her jumping half out of her skin and wrenching her neck painfully.

'Are you the one who brought in Seth Logan?' he asked, his tone so heavy with censure that her heart skidded.

'I came with him in the ambulance, yes,' she replied, half rising from the chair. 'How is he?'

He didn't answer. He was far too busy looking her over, his gaze no more approving than his voice. She tugged at the fringed hem of the silver dress even though she knew it ended a good two inches above her knees and had never been designed for so grave an occasion. Her silk stockings were torn and full of runs. She supposed it was from kneeling on the cobbled street and cradling Seth Logan's head in her lap, right after the accident had happened. Aware that her beaded headband had slipped a notch during the endless hours of the night, and that she looked incongruously out of place in the hospital waiting-room, she struggled to her feet.

He towered over her by nearly a foot, which made him at least six three. Compared to her winter-pale skin, his glowed from recent exposure to tropical sunshine. Hair as black and shiny as the rainy Saturday night outside tumbled in curly disarray over his forehead. His jaw, stubbled with incipient beard, bespoke authority and a stubbornness that bordered on intransigence. As for his mouth—even carved in disapproval, his mouth was beautiful, firmly moulded with the hint of a dimple at each corner.

Melody glanced away, appalled. What was she doing, allowing her thoughts to take such liberties, when a man might be lying dead down the hall, and all because of her?

'How is he?' she repeated, twisting in anxious fingers the long string of jet beads that dangled down the front of the silver dress.

He raked back the hair from his brow and flexed wide shoulders as though to ease the cramped muscles that no doubt came from spending hours bent over an operating table repairing the damage done to a body that had been run over by a limousine. He had good hands, she noticed, strong, long-fingered, capable, with the nails cut short and scrubbed immaculately clean. They added to his aura of power and she knew that, whatever the news, he had done his best. He was not a man who would give up easily on life, not his nor other people's. Seth Logan was in safe keeping—provided he was still alive.

'They'll be bringing him down from the post-operative unit within the hour,' he informed her coldly.

The air rushed out of her lungs in relief. 'Then he'll recover?'

'His leg is very badly broken in three places and he has multiple contusions. Given time and proper follow-up care after he's released, the leg should heal enough that he'll walk again—provided he doesn't develop pneumonia or a blood clot over the next few days.'

Melody shivered at the ominous words. 'And if that happens?'

'He'll probably die.'

She sucked in a painful breath. 'Oh, God!'

Eyes as coldly blue as Antarctica swept over her a second time. 'Very good, Miss Worth. One might almost be inclined to believe that you really care.'

She recoiled from the blatant dislike in his voice. He might be an excellent doctor and far too handsome for his own good, but if his attitude towards her was any example of his bedside manner it left a lot to be desired. 'I do care,' she protested. 'I care very much. When may I see him?'

'Never, if I have my way.' His gaze assessed her again, more scathingly than ever. He even had the audacity to hook a finger under the string of jet beads and reel her close enough for her to catch a whiff of his fading aftershave. The silver fringe draping her breasts billowed over the back of his hand in wanton invitation. 'The last thing he needs is patronising visits from someone like you.'

Fatigue and worry had her snapping back like an overbred poodle. 'That's up to Mr Logan to decide.'

'Precisely,' he agreed, a smile inching over his mouth without thawing the chill in his eyes. 'And Mr Logan has decided to send you packing.'

'I'll wait to hear that from him, if you don't mind.'

'You just did,' he said and, letting go of her beads, turned away dismissively.

Footsteps in the hall outside the waiting-room came to a stop in the doorway.

'Ah, you two have already met, I see.' The young resident who'd been waiting for the ambulance when it arrived at the hospital offered a brief smile and indicated the man beside him. 'This is Dr Fellowes, who operated on Mr Logan, Miss Worth. I thought you might want to have a word with him, since you were so upset when the patient was brought in.'

Melody felt her hand enveloped in a reassuring grip, and fastened her gaze on the person to whom it belonged. He fitted the role of surgeon, from the shapeless green garments swathing his body to the fatigue that shadowed his eyes. But in that case, who was the other man, the hostile one whose gaze continued to skewer her with arrows of condemnation?

'Why did you let me think *you* were the doctor in charge?' she asked, swinging back to face him.

'I didn't. You merely jumped to that conclusion.'

'Then who are you, and what right have you to tell me to stay away from Mr Logan?'

'I'm James Logan, his next of kin, which gives me every right. Miss Worth,' he stated, addressing the medical team in lordly tones, 'has been made aware of my father's condition, gentlemen. I hardly think you need waste anyone's time repeating what I've already conveyed to her, since she's merely a stranger who happened to be at the scene of the accident.'

'But a concerned stranger who might have questions of her own,' the surgeon suggested mildly. 'Miss Worth?'

Overshadowed by James Logan's scowling presence, Melody blinked. She wished she felt more in command of the situation and less like an errant minor brought up before an unforgiving judge. 'I—er—may I see him?'

'Not tonight, Miss Worth. He won't know you're there. But come back tomorrow afternoon, by which time he'll be better able to appreciate the sight of such a pretty young woman.'

The compassion in the surgeon's words and the smile that accompanied it had tears pricking at her eyes. She swallowed. 'Thank you, Doctor. You're very kind.'

'I told you, I don't want you hanging around,' James Logan growled as the medical team left. 'Go back to your fancy party and stop pretending you give a tinker's damn whether my father lives or dies.'

'The party's been over for hours,' Melody said, exhaustion sweeping over her anew. Sagging into the nearest chair before she fell over, she reached up and tugged the beaded headband from her hair. 'And even if it weren't, I couldn't face it, not now.'

He planted himself in front of her, cutting off the glare from the overhead light, but she could see him reflected in the rain-wet window at her side. A more disgruntled image was hard to imagine.

'It wasn't supposed to end like this,' she murmured, as much to herself as to him.

He smiled down at her unpleasantly. 'I'm sure it wasn't. How inconsiderate of my father to put such a damper on the whole evening when you'd no doubt planned to be the belle of the ball, sparkling with wit and dispensing charm to a host of admirers.'

'That's not so!' she protested.

Certainly, she'd expected she'd dance the Charleston, as promised, with flashy Roger who owned the shop next to hers in the Alley, and that the music and laughter would go on into the small hours. But her motivation for wanting to see the ball a success ran to something deeper than the shallow vanity to which James Logan ascribed it. A much more serious issue underlay all the hoop-la and glamour of the evening's festivities. What really mattered was raising enough money to turn a dream into reality.

Melody loved life, but then, why shouldn't she? She'd never known a day's need, never been shunned by those she loved. It grieved her to witness the despair of those around her who were less fortunate, and she found it almost obscene that she should have so much when they had so little. Establishing a soup-kitchen and drop-in centre for the unemployed drifters who hung around the bleak, cold streets because they had nowhere else to go had become more than her ambition; it was almost an obsession.

But instead of furthering the dream, what had she actually accomplished? One of those she'd hoped to help had ended up in hospital, worse off than he'd been before. 'No,' she repeated, her voice cracking, 'being the belle of the ball isn't what mattered at all.'

'Before you dissolve into tears,' James Logan warned her caustically, 'you should know that I'm immune to female crying fits, no matter how movingly they're presented.'

The unfairness of his remark revived her faster than apology or sympathy might have done. 'It seems to me,' she flared, 'that someone should be showing evidence of sadness or regret over your father's state of health, and, since it's obviously not going to be you, then it might as well be me.'

'I'm not responsible for his accident,' he pointed out.

'And I didn't arrange it on purpose! I wasn't driving the limo—I wasn't even a passenger in it! How was I supposed to know your father would get embroiled in a fight and fall into the path of an oncoming car? Come to that, why do you think the entire block had been cordoned off to begin with, if not to ensure the safety of pedestrians?'

'I don't know,' he said, 'but you can be sure I intend to find out. Until then, consider the subject closed, if for no other reason than that a hospital is no place for a shouting match, especially not in the middle of the night.'

She drew in a long, unhappy breath and pushed herself to her feet. 'You're right.'

'I usually am,' he replied smugly, and strode from the room before she could frame a rebuttal. Not that anything clever sprang to mind. In fact, she felt numb all over.

Because she had little option, she followed him. He stood at the end of the hall, waiting for the lift. She wished it would arrive and swallow him up before she reached it, but it didn't and she was forced to endure his silent company all the way down from the sixth floor to the lobby.

It was deserted at that time of night and so was the street outside, something which brought home to Melody the realisation that, in the confusion caused by the accident and getting Seth Logan to the hospital, she'd come without her evening bag or coat, and hadn't so much as a dime on her to call for a taxi.

James Logan operated under no such handicap. Indifferent to the rain beating down on his unprotected head, he strode to the edge of the pavement, stuck two fingers in his mouth, and let fly with a piercing whistle. Like magic, a taxi materialised out of the night and cruised to a stop.

He had flung open the back door and was about to slide into the warm interior when he happened to glance back at Melody shivering just inside the hospital entrance. At least ten feet of pavement separated them, but she saw the heaving sigh that possessed him.

'I suppose,' he declared with marked truculence, 'you expect me to be a perfect gentleman and offer you the first ride?'

If he'd shown the least sign that he had a chivalrous bone in his body, she might have responded differently, but his stoical certainty that she would live down to his every expectation of her stabbed her pride. 'I seldom expect miracles, Mr Logan, especially from such an unlikely source, so by all means climb into your taxi and be on your way.'

He actually hesitated for a minute, as if sorely tempted. Then another sigh rippled over him. 'You're turning into a monumental pain in the butt, Miss Worth, do you know that? Lucky for you, there's a shred of decency in me that forbids me to leave a woman stranded on a dark street in the middle of winter.' He swept an arm at the open door of the taxi. 'Go ahead and take the cab. I'll wait for another.'

When she didn't leap at his offer, he raised impatient brows. 'Well? Do you want it, or not?'

There was no help for it. She might as well throw herself on his already strained mercy, or else resign herself to spending the rest of the night huddled up on one of the hard vinyl couches in the lobby. 'I don't have any money on me,' she confessed.

He rolled his eyes, irritation evident in every fluid line of his body. 'It's on me, OK?'

She'd have loved to turn him down, but the cold was eating at her bones through the fragile stuff of her dress, making the beckoning warmth of the taxi impossible to resist. 'We could share,' she offered through chattering teeth. 'If you wouldn't mind dropping me off first, it would save you both time and money.'

'That's the first intelligent suggestion you've made all night,' he remarked, and jerked a thumb at the waiting vehicle. 'Now get in before we both drown.'

'Where to?' the taxi driver wanted to know.

'The old Stonehouse Mansion at the top of Citadel Hill,' Melody told him.

'Mansion?' James Logan's amazement was patently phoney and laced with ridicule. 'Her ladyship lives in a *mansion*, yet doesn't have the cab fare to get home?'

'I left my purse at the ball,' she said, 'but I'll gladly reimburse you the first chance I get.'

'Don't think I don't intend to collect,' he retorted.

'And for what it's worth, the Stonehouse Mansion was converted into apartments more than twenty years ago.'

He grunted indifferently and slid lower in the back seat, doing his best to stretch his limbs in the confined space. Making herself as small as possible, Melody absorbed the warmth emanating from him. The air smelled of sea-fog and winter, blended with the rained-out echo of her perfume.

She was aware of him watching her in the light of passing street-lamps. 'Why are you wearing this ridiculous get-up?' he asked, touching a finger to the fringe that spilled from her hem and sending tremors of warmth breezing over her knees. 'It looks like something from a 1920s Al Capone movie.'

'I thought you knew. We were holding a fancy-dress ball in the Alley.'

'The alley? You mean as in back alley, where the garbage cans and local drunks hang out?' He grimaced. 'The lengths the smart set will go to to get their kicks these days!'

'I mean Cat's Alley. Surely you've heard of it—anyone shopping for something special comes to the Alley's boutiques.'

'Boutiques?' The sneer was unmistakable. 'What was my father doing hanging around boutiques? The word's not even part of his vocabulary.'

Melody squirmed uncomfortably. She'd assumed that James Logan knew the full story behind the night's events, that the police had told him, or, failing that, someone from the hospital. She wished they had. In the face of his determined animosity, she didn't feel up to justifying the reasons that had prompted the fund-raising gala. 'He ... just happened to be in the wrong place at the wrong time.'

But something about her tone gave away her discomfiture. James sat up a little straighter and settled an unblinking blue stare on her. 'Why do I get the impression,' he enquired softly, 'that there's more going on here than meets the eye? What aren't you telling me, Lady Melody Worth from the Mansion?'

'Well,' she hedged, ignoring his sarcasm, 'I wouldn't have thought there was much left to tell. The whole town knew about the ball and that we hoped to raise enough money from the proceeds for...'

She dribbled into silence, uncertain how to go on, and stole a glance at James Logan. His raincoat was fleece-lined, his shoes hand-made Italian leather. What sort of son was he, that he allowed his father to roam the streets of Port Armstrong without a decent winter coat to his name?

'Yes, Miss Worth?' James Logan prodded gently. 'What were you hoping to raise money for?'

'Charity,' she mumbled, and wondered why the look he gave her made her feel as if she'd uttered a dirty word.

His attention never wavered and she knew with complete certainty that nothing short of a head-on collision was likely to deflect it. 'Charity for what?' he asked.

She waved a vague hand. 'Oh, people.'

'People?'

'I gather you don't live in Port Armstrong, Mr Logan,' she countered, deciding to match his aggression with a little of her own. She had done nothing of which she need feel ashamed, after all. 'If you did, you would surely be aware that there are some people in town who are...'

'Poor?' he suggested.

Sensing that she was treading on very thin ice, she chose her next words with care. 'Not exactly. ''Without hope or ambition'' would be a more accurate description.' And your father is one of them.

'And you thought you'd take it upon yourselves to make their lives more comfortable, did you?'

She didn't like his tone; she didn't like the relentless stare he fixed on her. And she hated the ease with which he soured good intentions with the taint of his scorn. She lifted her head defiantly. 'Yes, we did.'

James Logan's smile was full of malicious irony. 'It must be nice to have your own affairs in such good order that you feel qualified to meddle in other people's.'

The taxi, which had dropped into low gear to make the long, steep ascent up Citadel Hill, slowed down further to negotiate the turn into the Mansion's curving driveway and slid to a stop outside the front entrance.

'Actually,' Melody said with fresh dismay as another problem rose up to confront her, 'that's not exactly how I'd describe my affairs right now.'

'And why is that, Miss Worth?'

She glanced up at the imposing stone façade of the building, at its darkened windows and sturdy front doors hewn from three-inch-thick oak. The only visible light came from the gleam of the brass lantern hanging under the *porte-cochère*. 'I don't have my key to get in,' she admitted, in a small voice.

The rain drummed on the roof of the taxi and slanted dazzling needles of water in the beam of the headlights. James Logan contemplated them for several seconds, then fixed his gaze on her face again. 'Neighbours?' he enquired, without much hope.

She shook her head. 'The old lady who lives above me spends the weekends with her married daughter, and the couple on the third floor are on holiday in Tahiti.'

'And it would never occur to you to keep a spare key stashed away in some secret place, just in case you ever needed it?'

'As a matter of fact, it did,' she said. 'There's one under the flowerpot—on my balcony.'

Not a flicker of expression touched his features. 'And it, of course, hangs six feet above the ground.'

'About ten, actually,' she confessed.

'Which is undoubtedly my cue to offer to hoist you up and over the railing.'

'I'm afraid so, unless you can come up with some other solution.'

'Such as what?' he drawled. 'Offering to share my bed, as well as my taxi, with you?'

Melody's face flamed. 'Hardly! I'm not that desperate.'

'Neither am I,' he said, but appeared to put the lie to his words by running an insolent hand down the calf of her leg, then lifting her foot and settling it in his lap.

Her first instinct was to vent her outrage, her second to savour the suffusing warmth generated by his fingers sliding over her silk-clad ankle. 'I think I'll take these off,' he murmured.

She let out a breathless squeak. '*My stockings*?'

'Relax, Miss Worth, I'm referring to your shoes,' he replied, unbuckling the delicate silver straps across her instep. 'Your virtue was never safer. You're not my type at all.'

'Praise the lord!' she retorted.

'Nor do I trust you. I am not about to take a chance on your implanting your high heels in my skull.'

Frankly, she found the idea enormously appealing, but, as though he could see clear inside her head, he shot her a warning glance. 'It's not too late for me to dump

you on the front doorstep and leave, so what's it going
to be, my lady? Total co-operation, or abandonment?'

'I'll go barefoot,' she agreed grudgingly, 'but not until
the last minute.'

'Then let's get this show on the road. I've been up
since the crack of dawn and would like to catch a few
hours' sleep before the sun rises—assuming it ever does
in this God-forsaken part of the world.'

Opening the car door, he stepped out and reached back
to help her alight also, though 'yanking' was a more accurate description of the way he hauled her out. 'Lead
on,' he ordered.

Melody's heels sank into the sodden earth of the
flowerbed under her balcony. James Logan was pre-
dictably displeased to find mud oozing over the fine
leather uppers of his shoes. 'I should have followed my
first instinct and left it until tomorrow to deal with you,'
he muttered, disentangling himself from the branches of
a dwarf Japanese maple.

He wasn't the only one who was tired. It had been a
long and trying day for her, too. 'Oh, for heaven's sake,
stop whining!' she snapped. 'If it were my father lying
in a hospital bed, I think I'd be more concerned about
him, instead of feeling so sorry for myself. And that,'
she continued, as a gust of wind sent a sudden burst of
water streaming over his collar and down the back of
his neck from the gutter overhead, 'is my balcony, right
above you.'

'Terrific,' he snarled and squatted down. 'Get a move
on, and use my knee to climb up on my shoulders. And
don't forget to take off your damned shoes.'

With a little smile, she complied, and took the utmost
pleasure in planting her thoroughly muddy feet on his
expensive, fleece-lined raincoat. No doubt he'd present
her with a dry-cleaning bill in addition to the cost of the

taxi, but it was worth the price for the aggravation he'd caused her.

But he chose a more immediate way to get even. Straightening to his full height as effortlessly as though she weren't perched precariously on his shoulders, he used those fine, strong hands she'd admired earlier to boost her up and over the railing of her balcony with such energy that she toppled into a heap among the windblown leaves littering its surface. Her shoes followed suit in short order.

'I hope that you've stashed a spare key that fits your balcony doors, too, Lady Worth, because I'm not offering my services to haul you down from there,' he called out. 'There's a nice sturdy vine growing up the wall that'll make an excellent ladder. Shimmy down that, if you're stuck.'

And, clearing the flowerbed with a leap, her reluctant cavalier disappeared into the back of the waiting taxi and slammed the door.

He waited until the cab driver had rounded the first curve in the driveway before tapping on the glass partition and getting him to stop. Slewing around in the seat, he watched until a sudden shaft of light outlined a window beyond the bare branches of the trees. Thank God she'd at least managed to get inside without further incident. 'Bloody irritating woman!' he muttered.

'Lady get under your skin?' The driver grinned at him through the rear-view mirror.

'Like a burr under a saddle,' he acknowledged.

'Guess you won't be seeing any more of her, then.'

James wished that were so. There were other places he'd rather be, and other problems he'd rather tackle than those facing him here. And there were any number of people he'd rather have to deal with than Seth, who was a stubborn, bad-tempered man at the best of times. Heaven alone knew what he'd be like, laid up for a couple of months! But they were still father and son, whether either of them liked it or not. James supposed he had an obligation to go to bat for the old man and see to it that he was properly cared for and recompensed for his injuries.

But that meant getting to the bottom of Melody Worth's involvement in the accident which, in turn, unfortunately meant crossing swords with her again.

The cab driver braked to another stop at the end of the driveway. 'Where to now, mister?'

James contemplated going to the cottage and shuddered. Not tonight. Not yet. It wasn't his home, never had been. 'What's the best hotel in town?'

'Some might say the Ambassador,' the cabby told him, 'but I'd recommend the Plumrose. It's quieter.'

'Then drop me off there. I don't imagine I'll have too much difficulty getting a room at this time of year.'

For tonight—or what remained of it—all he wanted was a brandy, a hot shower and a comfortable mattress at his back. Tomorrow, he'd visit his father and reacquaint himself with a town that had undergone such a major face-lift in recent years that he had trouble recognising some of the old landmarks. Monday was soon enough to begin his investigation into exactly how Seth's accident had come about, and to make suitable arrangements for his post-recovery care. And it would be plenty soon enough to have to deal with her ladyship again.

CHAPTER TWO

SETH LOGAN was sleeping when Melody tiptoed into his room early the next afternoon. He was a handsome man whose features, even in repose, remained proud and strong despite the ugly bruise discolouring his temple. His mouth was firm, his jaw stubborn, and his brows bristled. Yet although she knew he was only in his early sixties, he looked old—old and tired, as if he'd led a hard life.

Carefully, she set a potted cyclamen and a basket of fruit on his bedside table. She'd been afraid James Logan would carry through on his threat and oppose her visiting his father, but she needn't have worried. There were no other flowers or cards, and no other visitors, nothing to indicate that Seth had a son, or friends.

Pulling forward a chair, she sat down quietly next to the bed and for a while watched the steady drip of the intravenous solution feeding through a tube into Seth's arm. Beside him, some sort of breathing apparatus hung from an outlet on the wall. A cage protected his damaged leg, which was immobilised through a series of pulleys attached to the end of his bed.

The silence unnerved Melody. She wished he'd wake up, so that she could see for herself that he was cognisant of his surroundings, yet, at the same time, she was apprehensive. She could hardly expect a cheery welcome when he found out who she was and what she represented.

She looked around, feeling useless as well as helpless, and searched for something to keep her occupied. She could top up his water jug, perhaps? Rising stealthily to her feet, she checked and found it had been recently filled with chipped ice. Outside, however, a watery sun struggled through the clouds to cast timid shadows through the windows. Deciding she could at least close the venetian blinds to prevent the light from shining directly on the poor man's face and disturbing him, she stole across the room and tugged gently on the cord that adjusted the slats. It was extremely reluctant to cooperate.

'You don't stop fidgeting with them blinds, girl,' a gravelly voice complained, 'you're going to have the whole dad-blamed lot coming down. Leave them be!'

Startled, she turned to find herself the object of Seth's bleary-eyed gaze. 'Mr Logan! I thought you were sleeping.'

'I thought I was, too,' he said, ''til you showed up and spoiled my peace. What're you doing in here, anyway? You're no nurse.'

She retraced her steps to his bedside. 'You don't know me, Mr Logan, but I came with you to the hospital last night. I was there when you had your accident. How are you feeling?'

'Like hell,' he informed her succinctly. 'How'd you expect a man to feel when he's been run over by a Mack truck?'

'Shall I ring for the nurse?'

'Not unless you think I'm dyin'. I don't trust a woman who takes pleasure in sticking a man full of needles!'

'But if you're in pain, Mr Logan——'

'I'm in pain, girl, mostly because I'm flat on my back with a headache, one foot hanging in the air contrary to where God intended it to be, and you keep calling me Mr Logan. Why?'

Oh, this man was going to survive! He was as abrasively strong-willed as his son, and then some! The knowledge cheered Melody immeasurably. 'What would you like me to call you?' she asked.

'Name's Seth,' he said, fingering his bruised temple gingerly, 'and the only people who call folks like me "Mister" are police, politicians and doctors. I don't trust any of 'em, so if that's your business you go back out that door and leave me to rot in peace.'

'I'm Melody Worth, I own a shop in your neighbourhood, and I'm here because I feel partly responsible for what happened to you last night. And I have no intention of being chased away so don't even try to arrange it.'

'Were you one of them who put together that fancy do in the Alley?' The blue gaze sharpened. 'You disappoint me, girl. You don't seem the type.'

She side-stepped the last remark. 'Everyone is terribly upset about your accident, Seth,' she said, leaning over to settle an extra pillow behind his grizzled head. 'The last thing any of us expected—or wanted—was for something like this to happen. But you're not to worry. One reason I'm here now is to assure you that I plan to take care of everything.'

'How?' a cynical voice at her back enquired. 'By smothering him with a pillow so he can't incriminate you with his account of what happened?'

'Well, lord love us all, look what the wind blew in!' Seth announced mournfully. 'You want someone you can call "Mr Logan", Melody, girl, you just found him.'

James Logan leaned in the doorway, raincoat slung over his shoulder and anchored in place by his thumb. Gone was the day-old stubble of beard and rumpled hair. Clean-shaven and with his unruly curls under control, he was possibly even more handsome in the clear light of day than she'd found him last night.

'How are you, Seth?' he asked, seeming not at all dismayed by his father's greeting.

'Laid up with a gammy leg and a sore head,' Seth replied, 'which is why I ain't high-tailing it out of here at the sight of you.'

'You've been a sore head for as long as I can remember.' James sauntered to the foot of the bed, a thin smile curling the corners of his mouth.

'Humph! Why'd you come?' Seth asked him dourly.

'Because I'm still your son, no matter how much either of us might regret the fact. When I get a call telling me my father's been injured in an accident, I feel an obligation——'

'You know what you can do with your obligations, *son*?' Seth sputtered. 'You can take them and——'

'Seth,' James interjected wearily, 'shut up before you talk yourself into a heart attack and put us both to serious inconvenience.'

Melody could contain herself no longer. Appalled at the exchange between the two men, she waded in to referee. 'You ought to be ashamed!' she scolded James. 'Your father's gone through enough in the last twenty-four hours without your speaking to him like that. As for you...' She shook her finger at Seth. 'He's right. Keep this up and you'll make yourself sicker than you already are.'

'T'ain't possible,' Seth muttered, glowering at his son. 'I just hit rock-bottom.'

'I think you should leave,' she told James in a low voice.

He took inventory of her sage-green leather suit, her Ferragamo handbag and boots. 'Do you?' he drawled and, like his stare, his tone was icy.

'It's upsetting him, having you here. Look how flushed he is. I don't think he's up to having visitors just yet.'

'And how did you earn your degree in medicine?' James asked witheringly. 'By clipping coupons out of fashion magazines?'

'I'm just thinking of what's best for your father.'

'You don't have a clue about what's best for my father, and I didn't fly halfway across the continent to take orders from a complete—not to mention unqualified— stranger.'

'You certainly didn't come out of concern, either,' she flashed back. 'It's plain enough that you're here under duress, and it's equally plain that Seth is no more pleased to see you than are you to see him.'

'Thank you for those kind words.'

Although his voice was controlled, something flared briefly in James's eyes that might almost have been pain. Too late, Melody saw that she had touched a nerve, and opened her mouth to apologise, but he forestalled her.

'Save it,' he said, sudden anger masking any other emotion. 'Neither you nor your sentiments have any place here, so get out before I really lose my temper and throw you out.'

It was not an idle threat, she knew. Scribbling her home telephone number on the back of one of her business cards, she tucked it into the basket of fruit she'd brought for his father. 'If there's anything I can do to make your stay here easier, Seth, please call me. And I *will* be back.'

With no apparent show of strength, James closed his fingers around her wrist and swept her towards the door. 'You can safely leave my father's care in my hands, Miss Worth.'

'Have you thought about the extent of his medical costs?' she muttered, wriggling unsuccessfully to free herself from his grip. 'The insurance might not——'

His expression underwent a subtle change, an edge of satisfaction softening the anger. 'I'm light years ahead of you,' he promised and, swinging wide the door, propelled her through into the hall.

They almost collided with a nurse carrying a tray which bore a hypodermic syringe. 'All visitors remain outside for a moment, please,' she ordered, then breezed into the room to enquire, 'And how are we feeling now, Mr Logan?'

Seth must have noticed the needle at once. '"We" are just swell, thank you kindly,' Melody heard him reply, 'so you can take that needle and stick it in your own backside because you're not getting anywhere near mine.'

Just briefly, amusement overcame Melody's irritation and, before she could stifle it, a giggle burst forth.

'Glad you've got such a great sense of humour,' James Logan declared grimly. 'Let's hope you don't lose it over the next few days.'

'Why should I?' she replied, rather more blithely than she actually felt. 'Your father's on the road to recovery, the sun's shining again, and, let's see, what else? Oh, yes! I found my coat and bag right where I left them last night, which renews my faith in the basic decent honesty of people and also serves to remind me...' she fished in her purse, extracted a bill and, reaching up, tucked it into the breast pocket of his smart navy blazer '...that I owe you money for the cab fare.'

James looked down at her hand with about as much delight as if he'd found a cockroach trespassing across his chest. She didn't even try to repress a second giggle.

His chilly gaze travelled to her face again. 'We'll see who has the last laugh,' he promised.

Refusing to show how daunting she found his remark, she favoured him with her sunniest smile. 'Try being pleasant yourself once in a while, Mr Logan. You'll be surprised how much better you'll feel, and how much more favourably the world responds. "Do unto others", you know.'

They were not empty words. Melody truly believed in them, modelled her life on their simple philosophy, in fact. Until she arrived at Cat's Alley on Monday morning, when it suddenly seemed that perhaps they were empty platitudes after all.

The other shop owners were all waiting for her beside the gazebo in the square—Ariadne and Chloe, Emile, Justin, Roger, and the Czankowskis—and it was apparent from their faces that troubles were multiplying.

'It's about time you got here,' Chloe, who owned the lingerie boutique two doors down, greeted her. 'We've got serious problems.'

'The Press has been on the doorstep since eight o'clock,' Emile Lemarques told her, his accent more pronounced than usual, a sure sign that the normally unflappable French-Canadian was perturbed. 'They are making much of what happened on Saturday night, Melody.'

'They want a statement,' Roger from the Crystal Palace told her. 'They're asking some very awkward questions, but we decided to hold off on any comment until you got here. How's the old man? Is he going to make it?'

'He'd better,' Chloe said. 'The last thing we need is to have our names blown all over the front pages of the *Port Armstrong Citizen*. I can see it now!' She flung out one arm. '"Undesirable dies under wheels of limousine at charity function". Hardly what you'd call good for business, is it?'

'You'll be thrilled to know that Seth Logan is alive and showing every sign of recovering, Chloe,' Melody said, making no attempt to hide her disgust, 'even if your concern for him does arise for all the wrong reasons. As for the Press, let them in and give them their statement. We've got nothing to hide.'

'Perhaps,' Emile suggested delicately, 'it would be best if *you* spoke to them, *ma chère*. The fancy-dress ball was your idea, after all.' He smoothed his already perfect silver hair and smiled persuasively. 'And you are so charmingly sincere.'

'Just don't make a mess of it,' Roger warned. 'We want to come out of this smelling of roses, not scandal.'

Ariadne yawned and rolled her magnificent Greek eyes. 'So much fuss about so small a matter,' she purred, offering Frederic Czankowski her sexiest smile. 'What can they do to hurt me, I ask you? Before Christmas, I sold enough furs to rich, unfaithful husbands trying to ease their guilty consciences that it doesn't matter if no one buys so much as another ear-muff until next winter.'

Seeing Anna Czankowski dart a suspicious glance at her husband, Melody felt she'd like to throttle Ariadne on the spot. The Czankowskis had arrived in North America as refugees from their native Poland twelve years ago, and had worked hard to make a success of their fudge and chocolate business. Neither of them had the energy or the inclination for extra-marital affairs, she was sure, but Ariadne teased Anna Czankowski unmercifully by flirting outrageously with Frederic the same way she did with every other man who crossed her path.

'We aren't all in your fortunate position,' she reminded Ariadne. 'Some of us need customers to pay the rent.'

Chloe raised carefully plucked brows in pained aston-
ishment. 'Oh, please, you can't possibly expect us to believe that! You were born, were you not, Melody, with
the proverbial silver spoon in your sweet little mouth?'

'Quit bickering,' Roger snapped, 'and let's decide the
best way to handle the vultures out there so we can get
back to business as usual. I've got a huge shipment of
crystal waiting to clear Customs, and I don't want it
hanging around gathering dust while the Press have a
field-day at our expense.'

'Then let Justin speak to them,' Chloe said spitefully.
'He'll get their sympathy faster than our rich little
brunette.'

'Sometimes,' Emile reproached her, 'you have the
tongue of a fishwife, Chloe.'

Justin Alexander rolled his wheelchair forwards and
peered through the grilled iron gates that separated the
indoor shopping arcade from the front lobby where the
administration offices were located. Just beyond, big
glass doors looked out on the street. 'We don't have time
for any of this,' he declared. 'Roger's right. There's a
mob out there growing larger and more restless by the
minute. Let's get it over with.'

'And let us all stick together,' Ariadne suggested,
sidling up to Frederic and tucking her hand into the crook
of his arm. 'What is it they say, darlings? "United we
stand"?'

'Your problem, Ariadne,' Chloe observed bitterly, 'is
that you never got saddled with a husband. If you had,
you wouldn't find men so all-fired fascinating.'

How was it, Melody wondered, turning away to unlock
the door of her own shop, that the plight of Seth Logan
and his friends so frequently took second billing to petty
disagreements like this? 'Am I the only one here,' she

asked, a distinct edge to her tone, 'who remembers why
we held a charity ball in the first place?'

'For appearances' sake,' Chloe said flatly, 'so spare
us one of your little homilies on doing kindly unto others
less fortunate. The bottom line here is what it's going
to cost us to keep these panhandlers away from our front
doors. As far as I'm concerned, the best thing that could
happen would be for the lot of them to fall off the edge
of the earth, but we all realise it would be politically
incorrect to say so in public.'

'I wouldn't go quite that far,' Emile objected.

'Nor would I,' Justin put in.

But they weren't willing to defend the underdog, either,
Melody realised. When it came right down to what mattered, Chloe was right. For most people, appearances
and the almighty dollar *were* what counted.

Leaving her coat and bag in the little store-room at
the back of her shop, she checked her appearance in one
of the mirrors then returned to where her colleagues
stood like guards at the palace gates prepared to ward
off attackers.

'What are you afraid of?' she asked them. 'Those reporters waiting out there to interview us are the same
ones who supported us with such favourable publicity
for the ball that all the tickets sold out within a month.
It's only natural they'd be here again now, waiting for
a news update.'

'God give me strength!' Chloe sighed, the irritation
that was never far from the surface boiling over. 'Is your
middle name Pollyanna, by any chance? They're blood-
hounds on the scent, and we're the quarry.'

Unfortunately, she was right, as Melody shortly discovered. A fair number of other people had joined the
journalists and the mood was indeed unfriendly. What
had been viewed last week as a worthy cause to help the

needy was now interpreted as guerrilla warfare on innocent bystanders. The shop owners' image had become tarnished overnight, their motives downgraded to pure greed and resentment towards helpless unfortunates whose only sins were the economic and social limitations forced on them by circumstances beyond their control.

'Seth Logan was run down in his own neighbourhood and might never walk again,' one reporter began. 'Is this your idea of reaching out a helping hand to people, most of whom were living here long before you decided to open a shopping arcade in the area?'

'Of course not!' Melody exclaimed. 'Mr Logan's accident was entirely unforeseen and we all regret it.'

'Not enough to dampen the party spirit,' a shabbily dressed man among the spectators accused. 'Things didn't wind down until four in the morning, as those of us trying to find a quiet doorway to sleep in know.'

'I can't comment on that,' Melody said. 'I spent most of the night at the hospital, waiting to hear about Mr Logan's condition, and I'm pleased to tell you that he shows every sign of making a good recovery.'

'Yet isn't it true,' another belligerent reporter asked, 'that you refer to Seth Logan and others like him as "the undesirables"?'

Dismayed, Melody cast a glance at her colleagues. She knew that Roger had coined the unkind phrase, but who had been so insensitive as to utter it publicly? 'That is not a term I have ever used,' she insisted, hating the fact that she could answer only half the question with complete truth.

A low mutter of disbelief rolled towards her. 'You don't like us hanging around here, though, do you?' a voice challenged. 'You'd like it if we were kept as far away as possible from your fancy little shops, wouldn't you?'

Wishing she could whole-heartedly deny the allegation, Melody hesitated, and looked again to her colleagues for help. None was forthcoming, but a disturbance rippled through the atmosphere as someone head and shoulders taller than most emerged from the shadow cast by a wrought-iron lamp-post set just inside the entrance to the Alley. It was James Logan, and he was all she needed!

As though he wielded some biblical power, the crowd parted for him to step forward, then flowed back around him, solid in their support for whatever it was he wanted to say. He didn't keep them in suspense for very long.

'Well?' he prompted. 'We're waiting for your answer, Miss Worth. How do you feel about "undesirables" frequenting your premises?'

'I've never turned anyone away from my shop,' she said.

'But are these so-called "undesirables" as welcome as your moneyed clients?'

The man was angling for a fight, encouraged, no doubt, by the rumble of support from his sympathetic audience.

'Look, Mr Logan,' Melody said, resenting the emphasis he put on the word 'undesirables', 'I've already stated that that is not a term I use, and——'

'But you don't condemn its use by others?'

Chloe, Ariadne and Roger glared at her from one side, and James Logan stared from the other. An expectant hush fell over the ranks. 'Yes—no!' she stammered.

'Which is it, Miss Worth?' he asked, in ominously gentle tones. 'Make up your mind.'

'I do not condone it. I think it's an inappropriate and uncharitable description,' she said, squaring her

shoulders, because there was no use fooling herself. His
expression remained impassive, but he knew he had her
trapped between the devil and the deep blue sea.

And what a devil he was! Great long legs clad in soft
wool, shoulders magnificent in a heavy fisherman's
sweater, and both hands shoved casually in the hip
pockets of his trousers, he still managed to look as if he
owned the earth and everything in it. Ariadne was
probably drooling.

Doing her best not to be cowed by his physical
presence, Melody sought to bring a satisfactory end to
the whole disastrous interview. 'Despite my personal
distaste for the term, I don't see it as my role to act as
other people's moral conscience and I refuse to be held
responsible for their indiscretions. My sole concern con-
tinues to be a fair deal for people who haven't always
been treated with the respect or kindness they deserve.'
She glared at her tormentor. 'And I think we all know
who I'm referring to, without any of us having to resort
to unkind name-calling.'

But she wasn't going to get away with things quite
that easily. 'Can we assume, then,' James Logan persisted, 'that, as far as you're concerned, the men and
women who have, for the most part, lived and worked
in this area all their lives are welcome to browse in your
shopping arcade any time they wish?'

Melody heard Chloe's hissing intake of breath, felt
Roger's growl of disagreement, sensed Ariadne's alarm.
Emile, when she looked at him, stood rooted to the spot,
clearly dismayed.

'What's the matter?' James Logan enquired with the
phoniest show of concern she'd ever witnessed. 'Are you
afraid your colleagues won't agree to that?'

What could she say—admit that they'd probably have
a collective fit, and thereby risk an even worse confron-

tation with this impossible man, with half the town as witnesses? How was that going to help matters?

She looked him straight in the eye and hoped she could be a convincing liar just once in her life. 'Absolutely not. My colleagues feel as I do. Anyone and everyone is free to come into our shops during business hours.'

'With no pressure from you to buy?'

'We never pressure customers,' she retorted, snatching a pitiful victory when it presented itself. 'The quality of our merchandise and service precludes the need.'

'May we quote you on that?' a reporter asked.

'Every word,' she replied, and from the smile that spread over the man's face he might have been a jackal moving in to pick over the carcass after the king of the beasts had eaten his fill.

'Then one last question, Miss Worth: why do the tenants of Cat's Alley feel these people, who you claim are far from undesirable, should be encouraged to spend their time as far away from your premises as possible?'

'I thought I'd already answered that question,' Melody replied. 'We don't.'

'Then why are you so anxious to have them relocate to the other end of the docks in what is currently an abandoned fish cannery? Could it be that you hope they'll be less visible there?'

More frazzled than she'd have believed possible a short fifteen minutes earlier, Melody combed distracted fingers through her fringe. 'That's not what motivated our concern,' she said. 'We were and are truly eager to contribute something positive to the quality of their lives. We're talking about subsidising a community hall, not a prison. And now, if you'll excuse us, shop-operating hours run from ten to five-thirty, and it's already past opening time.'

The other reporters shouted her down, firing a volley of questions.

'How much money did you raise?'

'What's it going to cost the taxpayer to have this facility built?'

'Who's in charge of the project, if it goes ahead?'

At her wits' end, Melody turned to her colleagues for help. Emile stepped forward, one elegantly manicured hand held aloft. 'Patience, *messieurs*! Be assured we will release a further statement when we have a better idea of how well our fund-raising efforts have succeeded. Until then, we have no further comment.'

'A fine mess you made of that!' Chloe informed Melody, as most of the crowd melted away. 'Not one of those grubby louts is setting foot inside my shop, and that's final.'

'They aren't coming in my place, either,' Roger declared gloomily. 'Can't you just see them, lurching around half drunk, and leaving a trail of smashed Waterford and Baccarat behind them?'

'Well, I'm sorry you're all so upset,' Melody said, annoyed by their reaction, 'but if you didn't like the way I was handling things, there was nothing to prevent you from stepping in and speaking your own minds.'

That put an end to their attack. They backed off, leaving her to sort through the morning's mail without further interruption. But her solitude was short-lived.

'I was almost beginning to feel sorry for you,' an all too familiar voice remarked from the doorway. 'I thought you were going to fold when those reporters started raking you over the coals.'

Of all the things she needed or wanted at that particular moment, James Logan's pity ranked lowest on the list. 'Believe me,' she shot back, 'after fielding your accusations, the gentlemen of the Press were a piece of cake, so save your concern for someone who needs it. And while you're at it, get out of my boutique. I don't carry anything big enough to fit your ego.'

'I'm not here as a customer,' James Logan replied, poking a curious finger into a silver bowl filled with dried lavender and rose petals. 'This isn't my kind of shop, any more than this is my kind of town.'

'What's wrong with this town—apart from having people like you inflicted on it?'

He curled his lip. 'It's too quaint to be stomached.'

'Oh, really! Well, it might interest you to know that it contains some of the finest examples of Victorian architecture in North America, and is considered a tourist spot well worth visiting for the glimpse it gives of life as it was lived towards the end of the nineteenth century.'

'Including this ridiculous set-up?' He swept an arm around, encompassing his view of Cat's Alley. 'Are you trying to tell me curly wrought-iron gas lamps converted to electricity are authentic? Or that Great-great-grandmother Worth kept tropical flowering shrubs alive in the middle of winter by computerised climate-controlled technology? And what about that bank machine so artfully dressed up as a brick wishing-well? Is that considered a mecca for tourists wanting to know how things were done back when Grandpappy was a shaver and running around in short pants?'

'No, Mr Logan,' Melody replied with severely strained patience. 'The merchants here have merely tried to preserve a very old warehouse and at the same time turn it into something practical and attractive, without detracting from the period in which the original structure was built. What you see out there is a faithful reproduction of a Victorian village square.'

'What I see,' he shot back scathingly, 'is a pretentious display of false fronts a lot like the phoney exhibition of concern you put on for the Press a little while ago.'

'I was entirely sincere, I assure you.'

'You were wriggling around like a fish trying to get off the hook, mouthing all the right words and looking suitably horrified at the suggestion that your motives weren't completely selfless.'

'And you'd have preferred me to appear unconcerned, perhaps, and thereby justify your determinedly poor opinion of me?'

'I'd have respected you for having the guts to be honest.' He looked her over searchingly. 'Tell me something: was this whole charity ball thing your idea, or was it a joint effort with the other shop owners?'

'A bit of each. I suggested it, but they all helped to put it together.'

'Reluctantly, I'm sure.'

'What leads you to that assumption? Are you psychic or something?'

He grinned mockingly. 'I don't have to be, my lady. When you were spouting off about anyone so inclined being welcome in your fancy little shopping arcade, one look at your colleagues' faces was enough to tell the whole world that the last thing they'll tolerate is a bunch of unwashed, semi-sober men tripping up their wealthy clientele.'

He was uncomfortably close to the truth. There had been numerous complaints that the presence of the 'undesirables' was spoiling the ambience of the area and discouraging 'decent' people from visiting the boutiques. It didn't say much for the generosity of a population that was, for the most part, very comfortably situated.

'You're wearing the look of a little girl caught with her fingers in the cookie jar, Miss Worth. Are you perhaps suffering a little twinge of guilt?'

The scorn lacing James Logan's voice in no way diminished the charm of its deep and lazy tone. For reasons she couldn't begin to fathom, Melody found her attention settling on such irrelevancies as the tiny nick his razor had left just below his jaw. It was the only flaw in the otherwise perfect skin on his altogether perfect face, an observation that caused a minor and completely untoward earthquake in the region midway between her stomach and her heart.

'Was there some more pressing reason that brought you here uninvited?' she enquired caustically. 'Or did you come simply to cause me added aggravation?'

The way he hesitated, his sudden smile that was all evil, dimpled charm and crinkled eyes framed by lashes that she'd have sworn were false if they'd appeared on a woman, set alarm bells ringing in her head. The man was up to something and, whatever it was, it boded ill for her.

He had his mouth half open, ready to reply, when the phone rang. Grateful for the respite, however brief, Melody reached for the receiver.

James watched her, resenting her fine, unconscious elegance. The graceful curve of her hand around the telephone, the angle of her head as she listened to the voice at the other end, the dark sweep of her eyelashes against her fine pale skin were things he'd have preferred to be able to ignore.

Worse, she reeked of money, the easy kind that he normally distrusted because it too often came accompanied by arrogance. Yet he couldn't shake the notion that, somehow, she was different. There was an air about her that he couldn't put his finger on. Not quite innocent, not exactly naïve, and certainly not unsophisticated, it had more to do with a quality of true honourableness, and it left him feeling like a class-one bastard because of what he was about to do to her.

He didn't want to be touched by her good intentions. It made more sense to be outraged at her patronising interference. Because of her, he'd been thrust into the role of concerned son towards a man who'd never wanted to be saddled with the obligations of parenthood. James despised the hypocrisy of the whole situation, so what was he doing, allowing this magnetic pull of attraction towards the perpetrator to take root?

The sanest thing to do was walk out of her shop and leave his lawyer to deal with her. There wasn't a single logical reason for him to have to confront her himself and risk any further involvement with her.

But he'd taken no more than two steps towards the door when he heard her soft gasp of dismay. Turning back, he saw that her other hand had come up to clutch at the phone and that she'd almost sagged against the glass counter. He didn't have to be psychic to know that the caller had disturbed her.

She looked up, and met his gaze with dark, troubled eyes. 'Mr Logan is here with me now,' she said, and unexpectedly James felt his heartbeat accelerate.

'Who is it?' he asked.

'Your father's doctor,' she said, and held the telephone receiver out to him. 'He's been trying to track you down for the last hour.'

CHAPTER THREE

JAMES'S hand was steady, his voice controlled, as he took the phone from her and identified himself. He listened attentively, then said, 'I understand. I'll leave right away.'

'Is Seth worse?' Melody almost whispered, as he hung up.

He shrugged. 'Don't ask me. You know how these doctors are; they never come right out and say what they really mean. They want to "confer" with me about the extent of his treatment. Apparently, he's not being very co-operative, which doesn't surprise me a bit. I suppose I'll find out more when I get to the hospital.'

She started towards the back room to pick up her coat and bag. 'Wait! I'm coming with you.'

'No, you're not. The only reason the hospital called you was because they weren't able to contact me at my hotel and they thought, correctly as it turns out, that you might know where I was. In any case, you have a business to run, and it looks as though your first customers have arrived.'

He was right. Clients who'd rented costumes for the ball were already showing up with the returns. 'Will you at least call and let me know how he's doing? Please?'

He shrugged impatiently. 'If you wish.'

She knew he'd rather forget she existed, and that the only reason he had agreed to her request was that he had more pressing things to do than get into another argument with her. Not bothering to say goodbye, he strode across the village square, his long legs eating up the distance to the front entrance at the far end of the Alley.

For the rest of the morning, people streamed into the shop, returning their outfits and lingering to chat. January in Port Armstrong wasn't normally a very exciting month, and word of Seth Logan's accident, coupled with the mood of the Press at the news conference, triggered an outburst of interest that wouldn't have survived the hour if they'd happened at the height of the Christmas season.

'You made the eleven o'clock news,' one of her regular customers informed her shortly before noon. 'My dear, I was shocked! Did you really invite *those people* into your shop?'

By that time, Melody was running low on tolerance. 'Which people are you referring to, Mrs Bowman?'

Her client tittered behind her hand. 'Why, "the undesirables", of course,' she muttered, sliding the words out of the corner of her mouth as if she feared giving utterance to the idea was all it would take to conjure up one of the unfortunate souls on the spot.

Inwardly consigning Roger to perdition for his unkind catch-phrase, Melody inspected the velvet bustle dress the woman had returned. 'One of the side-seams in the bodice has split, Mrs Bowman, and unfortunately the fabric is damaged. I'm afraid this is going to be a costly repair, since the gown is an original, not a reproduction.'

'I scarcely think it's going to matter,' her client retorted, offended. 'If you seriously intend to let common beggars paw through your antique clothing, it will *all* become worthless in very short order, and you can be sure I won't be patronising your establishment again.'

'I'm sorry you feel that way,' Melody said, and wondered why she'd ever thought the fund-raiser was such a good idea in the first place. At the present rate of progress, the benefits to those needing them most would be negligible, and the repercussions threatened to be every bit as damaging to business as her colleagues had feared.

James Logan's reappearance, just before one o'clock, did nothing to reassure her. Not for a moment did she expect that anything he might have to say would make her feel any better.

He lounged against the counter while she dealt with the last of the returns. 'Busy morning?' he asked, when the shop finally emptied and they were alone.

'Yes. How's Seth?'

'So-so.' He seemed preoccupied—diffident, almost—and changed the subject. 'What sort of business do you run here?' he asked, eyeing the pile of clothing destined for special treatment at the dry-cleaner's. 'A second-hand clothing shop?'

'You could call it that, I suppose,' she acknowledged with strained forebearance.

He wrinkled his handsome nose. 'And you have the nerve to call this an exclusive establishment? It looks like a lot of junk to me.'

Melody saw no need to pretend a politeness she didn't feel towards a man so thoroughly obnoxious. 'I stock classic clothing from the past, Mr Logan, but I don't expect you to appreciate either the quality or the worth. Just for the record, however, my inventory is extremely valuable.'

He shrugged, unimpressed. 'You don't say.'

She heaved a sigh. 'Let's not prolong the agony of this meeting. Why don't you tell me exactly why you're back here when we'd both prefer you were elsewhere?'

'I wondered if you'd care to have lunch with me.'

Her fragile composure disintegrated at that. 'Whatever for?'

He raised classically symmetrical black eyebrows. 'Because it's usual for people to eat something between breakfast and dinner. Does there have to be another reason?'

'In your case, yes,' she said, not about to be lulled into complacency by his sudden about-face. Brilliant blue eyes, beautiful mouth and tiny razor nick notwithstanding, he was still the same man who she was certain was up to no good. 'You're probably planning to lace my food with strychnine when I'm not looking.'

'Nothing so melodramatic, I promise. I just thought that, since we both have to eat anyway, we could share a sandwich while I fill you in on what the doctors told me this morning. And then, if you like...'

He flashed his dimples and tried to look harmless. If this had been her first exposure to him, she'd probably have melted on the spot. As it was... 'If I like what, Mr Logan?'

'Call me James,' he suggested cosily.

Not Jim, or Jimmy, or Jamie, but James—as in saints and kings. It was a small thing, but it sharpened her mistrust further. Adversary one minute, charmer the next, he was probably the most mercurial man she'd ever met, but two facts remained constant. He wasn't her friend, and he most certainly wasn't there to court her. 'If I like what, Mr Logan?'

'Well, we could perhaps visit my father together afterwards. He's being pretty unreasonable. In fact, the only person he's shown the least sign of tolerating is...' the smile faded a little, and James Logan swallowed as though something unpleasant was stuck in his throat '...well, is you.'

His eyes had taken on a smoky lavender-blue haze that softened their brilliance, and she realised that underneath he was very concerned about Seth, for all that he might pretend otherwise. Nevertheless, she was on the verge of telling him that, although she was more than willing to do whatever she could for Seth, she could manage to find her way to the hospital very well without James's company, when Ariadne came through the doorway, hips swaying seductively.

'Well,' she breathed, eyeing James approvingly. 'Well, well, well!'

Her husky tone, the gleam in her eye, the way the tip of her tongue peeped out to sweep hungrily over her full red lips, had the most astonishing effect on Melody. Just for a moment, anxiety for Seth took a back seat as a completely foreign emotion swelled up inside her. She recognised it immediately. Not normally given to jealous rages, she knew an intense urge to pull Ariadne's thick black hair out in handfuls.

Shocked and ashamed though she was, she couldn't help succumbing to a second, less violent compulsion. Scooping a dozen lace collars into a bag for hand-laundering, she smiled sympathetically at James Logan. 'Of course I'll come with you to visit your father,' she cooed. 'Give me a minute to get my coat.'

What happened next was no less than she deserved. The moment he realised he'd got his own way, his charm evaporated, which was probably just as well. It served as one more timely reminder that straight white teeth and eyelashes that curled like shaggy black chrysanthemum petals were genetic accidents, not character traits worthy of admiration.

'Don't take all afternoon,' he admonished. 'I've got a rented car illegally parked outside and I'm not trying to see how many traffic fines I can collect in this benighted town.'

Once they were settled in the car, he concentrated on driving his rented sedan along the tree-lined avenues that led towards the other end of town where the hospital sat high on a cliff overlooking the harbour.

'I'm curious about something,' Melody remarked, when it became apparent that he wasn't going to volunteer any further information about Seth.

To indicate that he had no wish to satisfy her curiosity, James gave a discouraging grunt—which she ignored.

'Why do we have to go together to see your father? If I didn't know better, I'd think you were afraid to be alone with him.'

They were approaching an unmarked intersection as she spoke. Up to that point, he had been driving with the sort of competent aggression she'd have expected from someone of his temperament—no hesitation about who had the right of way, no dawdling five miles under the speed limit. But her last observation had him grinding the gears and swearing copiously.

'You stalled the engine,' she said, with a smugness she couldn't quite control, as the car shuddered to a halt halfway through a right turn.

'I know,' he said, restarting the motor with a roar and grappling anew with the gear-shift.

'And you're holding up traffic.'

'How astute of you to notice.'

'Not to mention suffocating the driver behind with your exhaust. Do you have to rev up the engine that way?'

The car jolted to a second halt as he slammed on the brakes. 'Would you like to drive?' he enquired.

Melody smiled sweetly. 'Of course not, James. I'm sure you'll manage just fine once you regain control of your temper.'

'My temper,' he informed her savagely, 'is perfectly controlled, except when I run afoul of ditsy women like you who are enough to make a saint curse.'

The driver of the car behind gave a blast on his horn. 'You're still holding up traffic, James,' Melody reminded him.

'Oh, go bury yourself in a crinoline! And while you're at it, take your half-baked theories about my relationship with my father with you. I most definitely am *not* afraid to be alone with him. That's not my concern at all.'

Nor was it, as she discovered the minute she walked into the hospital room. It was a desperate bid to find some way to rekindle Seth's spark that had prompted James to swallow his pride and ask her to come back to his father's bedside. There was none of yesterday's fire in the sick man's eyes, none of the outrage at the unfairness of a world that had left him disabled and at the mercy of strangers he didn't trust. Even the sight of James provoked little more than a tired grunt.

'We came to see how you're feeling,' Melody said, taking his callused hand in hers. 'We hoped you might feel up to some company.'

'Not today, Melody, girl,' Seth replied, labouring slightly for breath. 'About the only thing I feel up to today is getting measured for my box.'

'Don't talk that way! James, come over here and tell your father not to say things like that.'

'Forget it, Seth,' James advised. 'Only the good die young, and you don't qualify.'

'Neither do you,' Seth said. 'Never will, either. Why don't you go back to wherever it is you came from and leave me to die in peace?'

'Not a chance,' James said. 'I'm staying until you walk out of this hospital under your own steam, so get used to the idea.'

A grimace touched Seth's features. 'Always were an ornery kid,' he muttered, then rested weary eyes on Melody. 'Been a long time since a pretty woman held my hand like this. Think you could stay a while after all?'

Impulsively, she rested her cheek against the gnarled fingers. 'All afternoon and evening, if you like.'

'Just a little while will do,' he murmured, his eyes drifting closed. 'Just a little while.'

Shortly after, he appeared to doze. For perhaps fifteen minutes, she stayed beside him. Then, when he appeared to sink into a deeper sleep, she tucked his hand under the covers. 'Let's leave him to rest,' she whispered, and turned towards James, expecting that he'd be only too glad to follow her out of the door.

To her surprise, he stood rooted to the spot, a look of utter desolation on his face. It was so completely at odds with his normal confidence that she quailed. 'What is it?' she whispered. 'You don't think he's going to die, do you?'

'Hell, no,' he said, hustling her out of the room. But his tone lacked conviction, and his eyes remained smoky with emotion.

'Then why are you looking like that? You're frightening me, James. Do you know something you're not telling me?'

He walked her down the hall to the lift. 'We're strangers,' he said, his tone bleak. 'We're father and son, and we're strangers. Not once since I arrived have we been able to...' He shook his head and looked at her, baffled. 'You walk into his life under the most adverse conditions and he gravitates towards you as if you were his favourite child, whereas with me . . .'

Then, seeming to realise how revealing the words were, he punched the call button with unnecessary vigour as though that might bring the lift to his rescue faster. 'Only Seth could be so contrary,' he said bitterly. 'Most men want a son, but it appears he'd have preferred a daughter.'

She saw that he was jealous and that he was hurting, and she pitied him. She pitied his father, too, because they were stubborn, proud men who didn't know how to reach out and help each other.

'If you told him you love him, he might feel differently,' she suggested, and knew right away that she'd have done better to keep her mouth shut.

'You've got to be kidding!' James exclaimed. 'I'd as soon face a firing-squad.'

'He's your father!'

'What's that got to do with it?'

'Everything.' She thought of her own experience, an only child growing up surrounded by loving parents, aunts, uncles and a flock of cousins who'd never allowed her to feel alone or lonely. James Logan probably wouldn't be able to understand what that meant to a person, but she wasn't going to let that stop her from pointing it out. 'Families should stand by each other, no matter what.'

His response was almost exactly what she'd expected. 'I don't happen to subscribe to that sort of pop psychology. I'm not about to be blackmailed into pretending an emotional attachment based on a genetic accident.'

'Then I pity you.'

'You *what*?' He was ominously, icily soft-spoken.

It was much too late to opt for retreat. She was up to her knees in a swamp of trouble, and could almost feel the alligator jaws snapping around her. 'Pity you,' she repeated recklessly. 'All that outraged male pride is more than misplaced. It's pathetic, and serves no purpose except to further your estrangement from your father. I don't know what caused this rift between you, but it obviously left you unable to admit to any feeling other than resentment towards him.'

His hand shot out and closed mercilessly around her wrist. 'You're wasting your talents hocking used clothing. You'd have three times more fun as a shrink, poking your nose into other people's affairs and telling them how to live their lives.'

Anger practically steamed out of his ears, but his face, she noticed, was ashen under its tan. Perhaps she had gone too far—for now. But she wasn't about to give up on him or Seth. They were two bull-headed men who refused to acknowledge the ties between them, and she decided in that moment that, even if her dream for the community centre failed, there was one thing she could and would succeed in doing. She would bring James and his father together, come hell or high water, because there was no reason in the world that Seth Logan had to be alone and lonely as long as he had a son.

'You're hurting me,' she said, in a pitiful little voice.

He looked horrified and dropped her wrist like a hot coal. 'I didn't mean to. I'm sorry.'

So he wasn't entirely lacking in redeeming graces! Without a qualm, she put her plan into operation. 'I think I'd like something to eat, after all,' she said, rubbing her wrist tenderly. 'Would you mind terribly if we stop somewhere for a sandwich before you drive me back to the shop?'

He glanced at his watch. 'Sure. Will the hospital cafeteria do?'

The food wouldn't be great nor the atmosphere conducive to the building of trust between them, but she had to start somewhere. For the next little while, at any rate, she planned to see as much of James Logan as it took to infiltrate his defences and persuade him to make his peace with his father. Never mind that she personally found the man insufferable. Enduring his company was a cheap price to pay to have father and son reunited.

'The cafeteria will do fine,' she said, and turned a deaf ear to the little voice of conscience that told her she was being sneaky. If she was, it was for a good cause.

It proved a remarkably easy cause to promote because, sadly, by the next day Seth had developed pneumonia in both lungs, and a week-long vigil at his bedside began.

'Isn't there some miracle drug to fight this?' Melody whispered, horrified that, in the age of modern medicine, a man's life should be threatened by so familiar an enemy.

James shook his head, his expression sombre. 'I don't think he cares about living,' he said, 'and there's no medicine on earth that can combat that.'

'Then make him care!' she returned fiercely. 'Hold his hand and tell him you need him. Tell him you won't let him just give up.'

But, as she already knew, that was asking too much of James. 'He'll know for sure he's dying if I do that,' he said. 'We've never been the kind of family that went in for that sort of stuff.'

Melody's eyes grew blurry with tears. 'Then maybe it's time you started, before it's too late,' she declared, almost choking on the words. Her initial plan hadn't called for such a blunt approach, but, with Seth's sudden crisis, she no longer had the luxury of time on her side. 'He's a lonely old man, James. If he's too tired to fight any more, don't let him die believing you don't care.'

'Of course I care,' James raged quietly. 'Why the hell do you think I came back to town in the first place? Because I can't live without his insults?'

She saw then that she was pushing too hard, that he was going through enough agony without added pressure from her. She slipped a hand under his arm. 'What I think is we both need a bit of a break and that it's my turn to buy the coffee,' she said. 'Come down to the cafeteria with me.'

By mutual consent, they fell into the habit of meeting at the hospital. Melody would stop by during her lunch break and again after she'd closed the shop for the day, and it seemed natural enough for her and James to share a quick meal together when visiting hours were over.

After a few singularly forgettable dinners in the cafeteria, however, and for the sake of a change of scene, Seth's night nurse persuaded them to try Francesco's, a small family-run Italian restaurant about five doors down the street.

'They're used to catering for hospital visitors,' she told James and Melody. 'The food's inexpensive but good, the house wine's great, and they understand that this is an anxious time for you and that you want to be left alone.'

'But what if Seth gets worse and we're needed back here?' Melody fretted.

'We'll phone,' the nurse assured her. 'We know the number.'

She was right about Francesco's. The music was low and unobtrusive and each table, set as it was in its own secluded alcove and illuminated by a single candle, invited the sharing of confidences.

At first, Melody did most of the talking—casual chit-chat about her childhood—but, as one day merged with the next and he seemed to relax around her a bit more, James started to divulge little snippets of information about himself.

'My parents were divorced when I was thirteen,' he volunteered one evening.

At his revelation, Melody twirled spaghetti around her fork and tried not to seem too eager to learn more. She knew he didn't share himself easily, and that it wouldn't take much to have him retreat into his old reserve if he thought she was prying. 'Did you understand why?' she asked.

He smiled with grim humour. 'Oh, yes! My mother recited all the reasons every day for the next six years.' He ticked them off, one at a time, on his fingers. 'My father was never there when she needed him—he was a commercial fisherman, did you know that? He preferred men's company. He wasn't a gentleman. He swore, he smoked, he drank with his cronies. Although sometimes there was money to spare, other times were very lean, but, either way, his first priority always was the upkeep of his boat. "Can't go to sea in a bath-tub, Susan," he'd tell her. "A man needs a boat he can count on when the weather blows up."'

Melody had lived all her life in the Pacific Northwest and knew well enough how severe the winter storms could be. Men and boats were lost every year, leaving behind families to grieve. It struck her as reasonable enough for a man to want a safe craft if he earned a living from the sea. 'But wasn't your mother prepared for all this from the start?' she asked James.

'Probably. One thing I have to say for Seth, he never pretended to be something he wasn't.'

'Then why did she go ahead and marry him?'

'She felt she had no choice.'

Melody looked up, puzzled. 'What do you mean—
"no choice"? Arranged marriages went out in the last
century.'

A glimmer of real amusement flickered in James's
eyes. 'Ever heard of a shot-gun wedding, Melody?'

She felt her cheeks flush pink. 'Oh! You mean...?'

He laughed outright then. 'That's what I mean. She
was pregnant—with me. She was only nineteen at the
time, and not at all prepared for the reality of being
married to a fisherman. The separations were hard on
her. She was miserable without him, but they fought the
entire time they were together, especially about money.'

'That's a shame,' Melody said. 'Money's not important enough to be worth fighting about.'

'Have you ever wondered where next month's rent's
coming from?'

'No,' she admitted.

'Then you're not in any position to know what's important and what isn't. Money always matters when there
isn't enough of it to go around.'

She supposed he was right. She knew for sure that
she'd hit a sore spot and that a change of subject was
in order. 'Did you see much of your father while you
were growing up?'

He shook his head. 'Very little. I lived with my mother
and we moved away to a town about sixty miles down
the coast where she got a job as a hairdresser. Seth would
show up once in a while during those first years, but the
visits always seemed to end in disaster, and eventually
he stopped coming.'

'He must have missed not being around to see his only
son grow up.'

'If he had,' James remarked stonily, 'he wouldn't have
allowed petty squabbles to keep him away.'

'He made a mistake which I'm sure he regrets. You might do the same, some day, if you have children of your own.'

'Not me,' James declared with daunting finality. 'I decided at a very early age to steer clear of marriage and the complications it brings—of which children are the worst. They make such ideal pawns when it comes to fighting dirty. Do you want dessert?'

'No,' Melody said, feeling unaccountably depressed.

Another time they went for a walk in a nearby park in an attempt to use up some of James's restless energy. The late January day was sliding into dusk, with a bitter east wind shredding the smoke from the pretty Victorian chimney-pots.

The park was deserted. Melody had expected they'd do a brisk circuit of the path that wound under the trees then head back for the warmth of the hospital, but, as they approached a children's playground, James grabbed her mittened hand.

'Come on, climb aboard,' he said, racing her towards a see-saw.

'It's too cold,' she protested.

But he refused to take no for an answer. Heaving her bodily on to the flattened end of the metal bar, he flung himself down on the other and set the thing in motion, swooping her up and down until she was breathless. By the time he'd dispelled all his pent-up energy and finally agreed to let her off, her face was stinging with the cold and she was sure her bottom must have frozen to the seat.

'You surprise me,' she giggled as they resumed their walk. 'I wouldn't have thought you capable of such . . . spontaneity.'

He'd been laughing, too, but at her comment his expression sobered. 'I suppose you find me very unsophisticated,' he mocked. 'I suppose you're used to more cosmopolitan types who find their entertainment in more glamorous pursuits.'

'Well, you're wrong, James,' she said, her own amusement fading. 'And I wasn't looking for a fight, so don't bother trying to start one. But since you brought the subject up, I wish you'd stop making assumptions about me and try asking me what I like and don't like, for a change.'

'All right. What sort of things do you like to do for fun?'

She thought for a moment. 'Dancing,' she finally decided, 'and eating. I love French cuisine.'

'Accompanied by champagne, no doubt?'

She rolled her eyes blissfully. 'I could *bathe* in champagne!' she admitted.

'That figures,' he said. 'How have you managed to put up with plain old spaghetti wine this last week?'

'The same way I've managed to put up with you,' she couldn't help replying. 'By taking the bad along with the good.'

It was a mark of their growing friendship, she supposed, that she was able to make that sort of remark without his taking instant offence, because all he said, quite mildly, was, 'You're a mouthy little brat sometimes, did you know that?'

'It's worrying about Seth that makes me sassy,' she said, shying away as he threatened to push her into a bank of rotting leaves, 'just as it makes you crabby.'

'Speaking of which,' he reminded her, 'we should get back and see how he's doing. I keep hoping that there'll be a change for the better, but he seems to be stuck in some sort of limbo.'

'I know.' Melody shivered, and not just from the cold. 'All that apparatus they've got him hooked up to scares me, and just watching him try to breathe is painful.'

'It's the waiting that's the worst,' James said. 'God help me, but sometimes I find myself wishing it would just be over, one way or the other.'

'Pray for a miracle,' Melody said, leaning her head briefly against James's shoulder.

'Not me,' he retorted cynically. 'I know better than to expect one.'

CHAPTER FOUR

A MIRACLE occurred the next day. Just towards evening and quite without warning, Seth suddenly opened his eyes and brought his gaze to rest on James and Melody.

'Lordy, lordy,' he croaked, his voice rusty, 'the death-watch committee has arrived!'

'Hardly that,' James said, and his voice too, Melody noticed, sounded suspiciously hoarse. 'You're not going to die.'

'Sorry to disappoint you, then,' Seth retorted, the ghost of his old fire surfacing. 'Who put this dad-blamed tube up my nose?'

'Visiting time's over, and I did, Mr Logan,' his nurse informed him, sailing through the door just in time to stop him from yanking it free. 'It's feeding you oxygen to help you breathe easier.'

'Well, take it away,' Seth demanded fractiously. 'And while you're at it, you can unhook this other contraption from my arm. I told you before, go stick your needles in someone else. I ain't interested.'

'Too bad,' the nurse said. 'You're obviously feeling much better, but everything stays put until your doctor decides otherwise. Now lie still while I give you a sponge bath.

'Relax,' the nurse continued, shooing Melody and James towards the door. 'You don't own a thing I haven't seen a thousand times before.'

'He's definitely on the mend,' James remarked with a slight grin once they were outside the room.

'Definitely,' Melody agreed.

They paced the length of the hall and came to a stop next to a rain-spattered window. 'Which means,' James said, tracing a circle on the glass and slashing a line through it, 'that you're free to spend your evenings doing the things you usually do, instead of racing over here the minute you shut up shop for the day.'

'Yes,' she said, wishing she felt more elated.

'No more hurried spaghetti dinners and cheap house wine,' James observed, sounding relieved.

He was smiling just enough for his dimples to show. His hair needed trimming. It curled a little against the back of his neck, which looked all the more tanned against his starched white shirt collar. 'That's true,' she replied gloomily.

'Back to your usual fare of champagne and French cuisine, I suppose?' he enquired, arching those fine black brows of his and stuffing his elegant hands into the pockets of his trousers.

'Definitely,' she agreed again, her fixed little smile in serious danger of falling off her face. The plain truth was that she found herself wishing Seth hadn't made quite so rapid and dramatic a recovery, and she felt like a toad. She didn't like to think she could be so small and ungenerous.

'It's raining pretty hard,' James observed, peering through the window. 'Is your car far away?'

'At the far end of the second car park, unfortunately.'

'How about one last lousy cup of hospital coffee to celebrate Seth's turn-around, then? Maybe by the time we're done the rain will have let up a bit.'

Exhilaration shot through her. She didn't care if it poured all night. 'I could probably stand one last cup.'

They found a quiet corner table and sat opposite each other. 'To Seth's recovery,' James said, raising his mug and touching it to hers.

'May he live to be ninety,' Melody added, and looked away because she was afraid of what James might read in her eyes.

He surprised her then by reaching over and taking her hand in his. It was the first time he'd touched her with anything approaching tenderness, and the shock of it tingled all the way to the tip of her toes in pleasurable waves. 'You've been pretty wonderful, you know,' he said, twining his fingers with hers. 'You haven't missed a day since he took a turn for the worse.'

'Neither have you,' Melody replied.

'I'm his son.'

'I'd like to think I'm his friend.'

'I think he'd like to think that, too. He's taken a real shine to you.' James let go of her hand and looped his other wrist around hers so that they held their mugs like loving cups. He grinned, bringing those disarming dimples into play again. 'There's life in the old dog yet if the sight of a pretty face can still stir him up.'

Melody felt a blush of delight warm her cheeks. 'Are you saying you think I'm pretty?'

A week ago, the question would have provoked him into irritation, and the best he would have offered by way of reply would probably have been something neutral, such as, 'Well, I've seen worse.'

Today, however, he indulged in a rumbling laugh. 'You know good and well that you're pretty, my lady, so stop fishing for compliments. It's not as if you care one way or the other what I think, after all.'

'You're right,' she said.

But she was shaken to discover that she did care, and that her lie caused a sharp, unpleasant pain inside. When she'd embarked on her plan to reunite him with his father, it had never occurred to her that she might end up falling victim to the charm James dispensed so sparingly.

'From the looks of it, this downpour isn't going to let up any time soon,' he remarked, nodding towards the window. 'We might as well make a dash for it now, and have done with.'

'That strikes me as a good idea for several reasons,' she said, and promptly wished she'd stopped to think before she'd spoken.

He looked rather taken aback. 'Such as?'

'I have things to do,' she mumbled.

'That's one reason. What are the others?'

She could tell him her private life was none of his business, something he'd have done without a second thought had their positions been reversed, but what had started out as a simple scheme to reunite a man with his father had hit an unforeseen complication.

She wasn't very good at dissembling, mostly, she supposed, because she'd never had reason to learn, so she opted for pared-down honesty. 'We're allowing our involvement to become too personal. We need to put a little distance between us.'

He stared at her. '*We?*' he enquired.

She'd wandered into that alligator-infested swamp again! 'I'm finding it less easy to dislike you, James.'

'Holy cow!' He sort of laughed. 'Should I be flattered?'

You could return the compliment, she thought resentfully. 'You're not exactly my type,' she said, 'and you've made it more than clear that I'm not yours.'

'We're in agreement so far. Go on.'

She heartily wished she'd never started. 'It would be easy, in the circumstances, for us to fall into the trap of thinking...'

'What circumstances?' He surveyed her narrowly. 'What are you talking about?'

'We've both been very concerned about Seth. Anxiety draws people close together, the same way grief does. But the fact is that you and I share precious little in common, James.'

'That doesn't mean we have to dislike each other.'

No, she thought, but it spelled disaster if the feelings ran deeper. Eventually she hoped to have a husband and a big family, with lots of children and pets, and it was obvious from the little he'd told her that that wasn't at all the sort of scene that fitted James's picture of the future. She didn't want to fall for a man who'd never make her dreams come true.

'Of course not,' she said lightly. 'All I really meant to say was that I know almost nothing about you, so it seems rather silly to——'

'You know I was a sad, misunderstood, adorable little boy,' he said, shrugging his shoulders and flashing her a dimpled smile.

'But next to nothing about the grown man,' she replied, hardening her heart. She gathered up her bag and gloves, and pushed back her chair. 'It's all irrelevant anyway, now that Seth's on the road to recovery.'

Heavenly days, she thought, preceding James out of the cafeteria, if she was going to act like a fool over a man simply because he had cute dimples and wonderful shoulders the less time she spent in his company the better!

But when they stepped out from under the canopy at the front entrance, the heavens opened with renewed force. 'Good lord,' James exclaimed, 'you can't walk anywhere in this! I'm parked just over there. We'll make a dash for my car and I'll drive you to yours.'

And at that, logic fled and she didn't have the will to refuse, any more than she had the strength to resist when he grabbed for her hand. Her fingers felt warm and safe locked in his, and it didn't matter a scrap that deep pockets of rainwater sloshed over her ankles as he raced her across the car park, somehow managing to haul her clear of the smaller puddles with the impetus of his long-legged stride.

'You look like a drowned kitten,' he said, turning on the inside light to unearth a package of tissues from the glove compartment when they were finally in his car. 'Here, let me mop you off.'

The soft paper stuck to her fringe, not nearly thick or heavy enough to soak up the rain dripping from its ends. 'Holy cow,' he marvelled, 'you've got enough hair here for three people.'

'It's nature's way of making up for the fact that it isn't curly,' she said, aiming for an insouciance that faltered abysmally when he grabbed another handful of tissues and, using both hands, pressed them like a helmet against her skull.

'How come you don't get it permed like other women?' he wanted to know, and his voice was husky all of a sudden, like smoke curling up into a cool October twilight.

'Because I'm not like other women,' she said on a frail breath.

He didn't reply for a moment, merely continued to hold the tissues close to her head, while his thumbs traced absent-minded little circles over her temple. 'I'd have to agree with that,' he said at last. 'You're definitely one of a kind.'

That was all he said, but she knew the words were the prelude to a kiss. She knew because the blue of his eyes altered subtly, matching the smokiness in his voice, and he promptly swept his lashes down to hide the fact.

She knew because she heard his quiet sigh, as though he wished to God he had the will-power to restrain himself, since giving in to the impulse was going to cause him nothing but a load of trouble he didn't need.

She knew because her heart raced out of time and control and she thought she was going to run out of air in her lungs.

And then all she knew was that his lips had covered hers and that they tasted sweeter than wine in autumn. She knew, too, that she had never been kissed like that before, nor had she ever responded in quite the same way. It was a devastating, shocking discovery, but that didn't stop her from kissing him back.

'This really isn't very smart,' he whispered, lifting his head enough for her to stare hazily at herself reflected in the dilated pupils of his eyes.

'No,' she agreed weakly. 'Someone might see.'

But that was rubbish. The windows of the car had steamed over and she and James were wrapped in a world as private as a boudoir.

'I should start the engine and get the defroster going,' he said, without a great deal of conviction. He even went so far as to turn the key in the ignition. But before the motor caught the radio came on, and suddenly the car was filled with the sound of Jeff Healey singing 'Angel Eyes'.

'Oh, brother!' James lamented, and brought his mouth unwillingly back to hers. The key dangled neglected in the ignition, while his hand slid around her neck and settled at her nape with warm, compelling insistence.

It was a different kiss this time, bolder and, if possible, more breathtaking than the first. It was intimate, invasive, the kind of kiss she never would have permitted another man on such short acquaintance, yet she submitted to him without a murmur. More, she returned the passion, answered the sudden hunger, and when his other hand stroked up her ribs to settle at her breast her only thought was that she had no idea pleasure could so closely equate pain and still remain exquisite.

Prematurely brought on by the dark clouds, night closed around them, enhancing their privacy. Chagrined, Melody knew that, if they'd found themselves in one of those large American cars with a bench seat and room to manoeuvre, she'd probably have let him make love to her. Fortunately, he'd rented a compact model, with bucket seats separated by the gear-shift. It was all that saved her. That, and James's exemplary control.

'This is undignified,' he decided, his voice a raspy, sexy whisper against her mouth.

'You're right,' she whispered back, and blinked, unable to believe how much it hurt her that he wasn't so driven by desire that he could consign dignity to perdition.

He started the car, turned the defroster up full-blast, and fiddled with the radio tuner to find a news station. 'Rain, rain, and more rain,' the announcer predicted. 'Flooding is expected in low-lying areas, and gale-force winds are forecast for the Strait.'

Melody's spirits felt as darkly depressed as the weather. When had her emotions become so entangled, and what in the world had possessed her, that she could let herself get so carried away by a kiss?

When his car drew up next to hers, she muttered a hurried 'Goodbye, thanks for the ride' and swung open the door. It was obvious from his silence during the brief ride that James had nothing further to say to her and that he regretted his brief lapse into madness. She wasn't about to linger and afford him the opportunity to tell her so.

'So long,' he said, and didn't even bother to wait until she'd started her own car's engine before spraying a tide of water over her windscreen with the speed of his exit from the car park.

She felt like crying. She must be insane!

He must be insane! What had possessed him? Had it been the sight of her dripping wet with her hair as darkly sleek as a seal's? Or had it been her lashes fluttering against *his* cheek as they swept down to hide those big, beautiful eyes of hers that reminded him of wide-faced pansies sewn out of soft black velvet? Or was it just that her perfume had intensified to hypnotic proportions in the steamy interior of the car, luring him to foolish actions with disastrous consequences?

Good God, he was waxing poetic—he, whose entire professional life was governed by the dynamics of angles and curves as they pertained to the blueprints of ship design! Even as a child, he'd been a pragmatist, having learned early and well that dreamers were rewarded with little but disappointment. So what was he doing now, at thirty-four, acting like a foolish romantic and necking with a woman he barely knew—in a public place, too?

There was absolutely no logical reason to feel drawn to her. Anything but! He'd met enough types like her to know where their priorities lay. They wanted rich husbands to support their expensive tastes, and, if he'd occasionally wondered if she might have different ambitions, everything new he discovered about her was enough to tell him otherwise. This lady wasn't used to settling for anything less than the best.

Once back at the Plumrose Hotel, he checked up on his messages, then flung himself full-length on the king-size bed in his suite and stared moodily at the frescoed ceiling, furious at the mental image that superimposed itself on the dimpled cherubs overhead. It was too easy to imagine her sprawled out beside him, midnight hair spilling over her forehead, midnight eyes inviting him, sweet pink mouth tempting him.

Just briefly, he'd toyed with the idea of luring her back to his room for a night-cap, with the express intention of making love to her again and again. But he'd known just as surely that it would have been a mistake.

He didn't like making mistakes. He found it much too hard owning up to them.

Because things were quiet in Cat's Alley the next morning, Melody decided to change her window display. Lace Victorian hearts seemed appropriate, with Valentine's Day only two weeks away. Just because she couldn't drum up any enthusiasm for celebrating didn't mean the rest of the world wanted the occasion to go ignored.

She was busy scattering posies of dried flowers along the hem of a late-nineteenth-century wedding-gown when Chloe rapped on the plate glass and popped her head around the door. 'You've got company,' she informed Melody tartly, 'and I don't imagine you need an introduction to guess who they are.'

Roger's head joined Chloe's. 'Get rid of them, kiddo. They don't make good window-dressing.'

Four or five men stood shuffling their feet uneasily a few yards away. Hands jammed in the pockets of their ill-fitting overcoats, they appeared to be debating the wisdom of coming any closer.

'They're——' Melody began.

'Undesirables,' Roger finished for her. 'I wouldn't let them inside the shop, if I were you. They've got that light-fingered look about them.'

'Down-hearted and hungry strikes me as a better description,' she muttered, slipping her shoes back on and going out to meet them.

'We aren't here to make trouble,' one of them began defensively, at her approach. 'We just wanted to ask how Seth Logan's doin'. We know you go to see him all the time.'

'He's much better,' Melody was glad to be able to tell them. They looked as if they could use a bit of good news for a change.

'We reckoned he wasn't coming out of that hospital alive,' another said. 'Seth ain't the type to lie around in bed if he's got any say in the matter.'

Melody smiled. 'He hasn't been given much choice so far, but I don't expect that to last much longer.'

'The boys...' The first spokesman frowned uncertainly. 'Well, we wondered, is there anything we can do for him? We don't have much, but we've been buddies a long time and we'd like to help him out, if we can.'

'I think he'd enjoy a few more visitors,' she said. 'It would help pass the time for him, and I'm sure he'd be glad to see you.'

Just then, a younger couple approached. The man, probably in his early forties, looked vaguely familiar. 'We're from the local TV station, Miss Worth,' the woman said, handing Melody a business card, 'and we wondered if you'd agree to an interview on *City Streets* next Tuesday evening. As you probably know, it's a weekly talk show that spotlights items of public interest in Port Armstrong, and your name's been in the news quite a lot recently.'

'We'd like to do a feature on your idea for setting up a community centre in the dock area,' the man, whom Melody now recognised as the host of the TV show in question, explained. 'Make the public more aware of the problem, if you understand what I mean. By the way, I'm Don Hellerman.'

What Melody understood was that Seth's friends had melted away like fog in July the minute the topic of the centre had come up, and that they had been replaced by Chloe, Roger, Ariadne and Emile. Justin and the Czankowskis, though no less interested, maintained a more discreet distance. 'I know who you are,' she told Don Hellerman, 'but I'm not sure I know what you mean by "problem". Are you talking about the idea itself, or the people it's intended for?'

'Miss Worth,' Don Hellerman replied smoothly, 'you can use the show as a platform for dealing with the subject any way you feel will best serve public interest. I never try to programme my guests ahead of time.'

Remembering their reaction the last time she'd acted as spokesperson for them, Melody turned to her colleagues. 'I think this is something that we should all have a say in. How do you feel about it?'

'It's your baby,' Roger said hastily, backing away. 'Has been from the very start. Deal with it any way you want.'

'Within reason,' Chloe interjected, not quite as willing to give her free rein. 'Remember we all have to live with what you say.'

Don Hellerman's beady little eyes gleamed. 'If there's a difference of opinion,' he said, flashing expensively capped teeth at Ariadne, 'I can accommodate more than one guest on the show.'

'I'm available,' Ariadne breathed.

'But not required,' Emile cut in. '*Monsieur*, we are of one accord. Miss Worth is our chosen representative.'

Moving closer, Justin and Frederic Czankowski added their voices, with Anna nodding support. 'Thanks for the vote of confidence,' Melody said, once the television personalities had left. 'I wish I felt it was more unanimous, though.'

'We all support you, *ma chère*, and if there is one among us who would disagree with that let him step forward and offer to take your place,' Emile said.

'Don't look at me,' Roger warned him. 'I'm not making a fool of myself in front of the whole of Port Armstrong. If Melody wants the job, she's got it, as far as I'm concerned.'

'I'm not sure I do want the job,' Melody said. 'For a start, there's something about that Don Hellerman that I don't quite trust. In fact, he gives me the creeps. But I didn't want to give him any reason to think we were backing off about the importance of supporting the community centre.'

'You had no choice but to agree to the interview,' Justin assured her. 'And let's face it, donations have dropped off in the last week or so. People forget about things like this, if you don't frequently remind them.'

'We could forget about it, too,' Chloe said. 'If you ask me, that's the best idea of all.'

'Unfortunately, we don't have that choice any more,' Justin said. 'We've already collected a fair bit of money, and we can't just pocket it and conveniently forget why we asked for it in the first place. We'd be up on charges of theft and fraud before we had time to hire ourselves a lawyer.'

'I'm not happy about any of this,' Chloe persisted. 'I've said from the beginning, it was a big mistake getting involved in such a daft scheme.'

'What would it take to make you happy about anything?' Roger snorted.

'A sweet, sympathetic, virile man,' Ariadne purred, batting her eyelashes at Frederic. 'Whether or not our

Chloe will admit it, she is withering for lack of male attention.'

Frustration had Melody grinding her teeth as the conversation degenerated into the sort of personal attacks that were becoming an altogether too frequent occurrence for her peace of mind. 'It's just as well you don't want to go on TV to air your views,' she told Ariadne, Chloe and Roger. 'Let the three of you loose, and the interview would be a guaranteed disaster. I might not always say what you think I ought to say, but at least I know enough to stick to what's important and not allow myself to get side-tracked by petty issues.'

It was a boast she lived to regret. Before the interview was half over the following Tuesday, Melody suspected she'd single-handedly managed to do more damage than Roger, Chloe and Ariadne at their collective worst. From the minute she set foot inside the television studio, things went wrong.

For a start, the very junior assistant who greeted her was appalled by Melody's request to meet with Don Hellerman before the show went on the air.

'I couldn't possibly disturb Mr Hellerman during make-up,' the girl insisted. 'He would be very annoyed.'

'I'm very annoyed,' Melody informed her. 'Mr Hellerman hasn't bothered to return any of several calls I've made to him since he convinced me to appear on his show, and I'd like the chance to discuss with him ahead of time the sort of questions he's likely to be asking.'

'I'll see what I can do,' the assistant promised, and fled the scene, leaving Melody to stew in splendid isolation in a cubicle the size of a shower cubicle.

The last few days hadn't been among the most enjoyable in her life. Her hours at the shop had been slow

enough, but that had palled beside the dragging mon-
otony of the evenings and weekend. Nothing on her
social calendar had seemed worth getting excited about,
mainly, she was forced to admit, because Don Hellerman
wasn't the only one who hadn't bothered to pick up the
phone and give her a call. James Logan had been con-
spicuous by his silence too, and she was having a hard
time coming to grips with the unhappiness his neglect
was causing her.

When the junior assistant finally reappeared, it was
only to announce, 'You're on in three minutes, Miss
Worth. If you'll come with me, I'll show you where to
wait for your introduction.'

Obviously Don Hellerman had no intentions of
affording his guest a few minutes of his precious time,
and the sinking feeling that had begun the day she had
agreed to the interview deepened in Melody's stomach.

The studio was a maze of trailing electrical cords and
cameras. Bright lights illuminated a corner where the TV
host whined petulantly while someone from the make-
up department fiddled with his thinning hair. Beyond
the glare, Melody could vaguely discern tiers of seats
and hear the murmur and rustle of a live audience.

'Thirty seconds,' someone called out and suddenly
Melody forgot about everything, even James. In fact her
mind drew a complete blank as the most overpowering
attack of nerves she'd ever experienced overtook her.

Music mixed with orchestrated applause drowned out
the hammer of her heart. Don Hellerman assumed his
familiar urbane manner, speaking to the camera as if it
were an old and beloved friend. '*City Streets*, ladies and
gentlemen, the programme that——'

The junior assistant prodded her gently in the spine.
'Any minute now, Miss Worth.'

'Converting an abandoned fish cannery three blocks removed from the shopping arcade. A worthy cause, on the surface, but what really motivates this group of tenants from Cat's Alley? Humanitarianism—or avarice?' The mellifluous voice floated out across the audience. 'Let's find out. Please welcome my first guest, Miss Melody Worth.'

Propelled from behind, and half blinded by the lights in front, Melody stepped before the cameras to a round of lukewarm applause. Her first instinct was to march up to the TV host and slap him for his nasty innuendoes, but sanity warned her that she'd be playing directly into his hands if she gave in to the urge. Unless she took charge of her emotions, Don Hellerman would have little trouble making her look like a mindless goose.

'Miss Worth, tell us all why you're so committed to this idea of opening a community centre for residents of the area where you work.'

'Because I see the need for one,' she said bluntly, deciding that brevity would get her into less trouble than waxing eloquent.

'And what exactly would you like to see in this so-called centre?'

'A kitchen supplying cheap, nutritious meals for those unable to cook for themselves. A reading room with comfortable chairs and a fireplace, where a person can read the newspapers. A games room, with billiards and shuffleboard. In other words, a place where people can meet and enjoy each other's company.' She paused to draw breath. 'And a dormitory, where a person can find a clean bed for the night if it's required.'

Hellerman raised his brows and plastered his hair more closely to his scalp. 'Are you talking about a shelter and soup-kitchen, Miss Worth?' he asked doubtfully.

'Call it what you like,' Melody replied. 'What matters is that there's a crying need for a facility such as I've described. There are too many people practically living on the streets.'

'By that, you mean people who are underprivileged?'

'In one way or another, yes.'

Hellerman stroked his chin lovingly. 'And how did you arrive at that conclusion, my dear young lady?'

'Mr Hellerman,' Melody replied tartly, thoroughly ticked off at his patronising tone, 'what other conclusion is there when all an intelligent person has to do is look outside on a raw winter's day and see men huddled in shop doorways to avoid the bitter weather?'

The ripple of applause from the audience might have warmed her, had not the sudden tightening around the host's mouth told her she'd made a serious error in assuming that he would tolerate being upstaged by one of his guests. Fixing her in cold stare, he abruptly changed the subject. 'You were born in the house which your parents still own on two acres of waterfront property in the old and prestigious Pacific Heights district of Port Armstrong. You grew up in the care of a nanny, and later were sent to private schools, first in this country, and later in Switzerland, where you completed your education.'

'I attended university in the United States before going to Switzerland,' she interjected, unwilling to forgo the chance to set him straight on at least one small omission. He had obviously researched her very thoroughly and probably knew that two of her molars had fillings.

Don Hellerman waved a dismissing hand. 'No matter. When you returned to Canada, you opened your own shop on Main Street, and relocated your business to Cat's

Alley when it was converted into a shopping arcade. Tell us about your shop, Miss Worth.'

'It's called Yesteryear,' Melody said, 'and I stock period clothing which I rent out to private parties, museums, theatre groups and the like.'

'An essential service, I'm sure,' Don Hellerman smirked, 'and one which leaves you time to organise fund-raising events such as your costume ball in January—an event, incidentally, from which you personally must have profited considerably. How much money did you take in on rentals for that night, Miss Worth?'

For a moment, Melody stared at him, astounded at the gall of his insinuations. Then, collecting her wits, she replied very distinctly, 'I'm sure you will forgive me for not answering that question, Mr Hellerman, just as I will forgive you for having been so unforgivably rude as to ask it.'

Another grievous error! 'You seem to be rather sensitive to invasions of privacy,' he returned suavely, 'at least when it's your privacy that's being invaded. That strikes a somewhat ironical note, don't you think, considering your lack of sensitivity towards other people's right to the same privilege?'

'I'm not sure what you're driving at,' she snapped.

'Then perhaps I should introduce my second guest,' he said, addressing the audience. 'I'm sure when we hear what he has to say we'll all know exactly what I'm driving at.'

If ever she'd had cause to doubt its existence, Melody knew in that instant that women's intuition amounted to a lot more than a myth. The hair on the back of her neck stood up, and a dreadful certainty swept over her.

She didn't need to look around to know who was striding purposefully on to the set from the opposite side.

'Ladies and gentlemen, please welcome James Logan, one of Port Armstrong's native sons,' Don Hellerman invited.

He took a chair on the other side of the unpleasant Mr Hellerman. He stretched his long legs out and crossed them at the ankles. He leaned on one elbow, and nodded briefly at the TV host. And even though her outraged stare ought to have burned holes in his skull, not once did James so much as glance at her.

She knew without a shadow of doubt that he'd come prepared to do battle, that she had been selected as his adversary, and that he had no intention of retiring undefeated.

She felt like a hapless Christian about to be thrown to the lions.

CHAPTER FIVE

THINGS deteriorated rapidly after that.

'Did you grow up in Pacific Heights too, Mr Logan?' Don Hellerman asked, with about as much innocence as a rattlesnake poised to strike.

James allowed himself a brief, unamused smile. 'No. I was born at the other end of town—Sailors' Reach, to be precise—though it goes under a different name these days, ever since it's become a popular stamping ground for the smart crowd.'

'It would be fair to say, then, that you were from the wrong side of the tracks?'

'I don't know that I'd call it fair,' James said. 'The area had more than its share of bars and dives, but you expect that in any sea port, however small. I never went to bed hungry.'

'But you didn't have a nanny, I bet.'

Again that small, ironic smile. 'No. Good help was hard to find in our neck of the woods.'

A burst of sympathetic laughter rose from the audience. Hellerman wasted no time cashing in on it. 'I imagine the same could be said of private schools.'

'Oh, a few of the kids I knew ended up in private institutions—of a sort.'

'But not the kind Miss Worth is familiar with, I'm sure.'

For the first time, James deigned to glance at Melody. 'No,' he agreed. 'She looks pretty law-abiding to me.'

He looked gorgeous, all polished ebony and bronze.

'You're a naval architect, I believe. Won a full scholarship to an excellent university.' Don Hellerman referred to the printed notes on the low table in front of him. 'Graduated *summa cum laude*, apprenticed with the most respected firm of naval architects on the eastern seaboard. Started your own company five years ago. Touted in a national news magazine as one of the up-and-coming independent businessmen to be reckoned with, received the yacht-racing-award for best design of the year. Not bad, for a boy who grew up on the less privileged side of town.'

'Thank you.' James inclined his head graciously.

Gorgeous or not, Melody wanted to shake him.

'And definitely a man who knows how both halves live. So tell me, James——' Don Hellerman lowered his voice to the confiding 'just between us men' sort of tone Melody associated with smoky bars and sexist jokes '—what do you think of this little lady's idea to convert an old fish cannery to a soup-kitchen-cum-shelter that will keep people from your old neighbourhood off the streets?'

'I think it stinks—of something other than fish,' James said, and earned a burst of applause and laughter from the audience for his wit.

She was wrong, Melody decided. She didn't want to shake him; she wanted to choke him. Slowly. One breath at a time.

Hellerman tried to look guileless as he gazed at the camera, but it was a wasted effort as far as Melody was concerned. 'Why do you say that, James?'

'Because the people she thinks ought to take advantage of it won't give her a thank-you for it.'

'How do you know?' Melody snapped, tired of being treated as if she were of such little consequence that she was beneath notice. 'Have you asked them?'

'I don't need to,' James said. 'I know how they feel. They don't want your charity. They resent it. Furthermore, it does nothing to resolve the underlying problems.'

'What problems?' Hellerman enquired, clearly delighted at the combative attitude that had sprung up between his guests.

'Feeling useless. These aren't people who choose to be idle; they've been rendered redundant by the new society that has shaped this town,' James declared, with an unmistakable ring of sincerity. 'Shelters and soup-kitchens are band-aid solutions to a problem that goes much deeper. These are men and sometimes women, too, who want to be a part of life in that section of town that's always been their home. They want to contribute.'

'But all Miss Worth wants, it seems, is to have them shunted out of sight,' Hellerman said, 'which brings me back to my question this evening: what really motivates the drive behind this project—compassion, or avaricious snobbery?'

'If that's your only reason for asking me to appear as your guest,' Melody informed him, 'then you're probably leaving yourself open to a lawsuit for infringement of copyright, since all you've done so far is parrot what you obviously read in the local newspaper a few weeks ago. And even if they don't sue you, I just might.'

'Now just hold on a moment, Miss Worth!'

'No, you hold on a moment, because I'm not finished. First of all, the very least you can do is afford me equal air time, but since you're much more concerned with getting maximum mileage out of a lot of sensational innuendoes that bear no resemblance to the truth than you are in giving me a fair hearing I see no reason to remain here. I don't get paid to keep viewers entertained at any cost, Mr Hellerman, you do. So it doesn't matter a rap to me if you're left with empty air space. Fill it with more of your scandalmongering rubbish, for all I care.' She flung a withering glance at James Logan, who had the nerve to sit there with a rather pleased grin on his face. 'Heaven knows, your other guest seems more than willing to put in his two bits' worth to help you out if you happen to run dry!'

'The little lady speaks of litigation!' Hellerman exclaimed, appealing to the audience. 'The very same little lady who, if my sources are correct, stands in danger of being sued herself...' he paused for added dramatic effect '...by none other than my second guest! And why? Because, even as we speak, James Logan's father lies crippled in a hospital bed because of the Cat's Alley tenants' determination to rid the streets around their premises of what they call "the undesirables". Seth Logan, who only a few short weeks ago was as active as anyone here, has been left permanently maimed and unable to care for himself! Now if *that* doesn't paint a more accurate picture of what's really going on here, ladies and gentlemen, what does?'

Melody didn't dwell on the fact that the TV host was mouthing more outrageous lies about Seth. She was too stunned at his revelation of James's intentions. 'You had the nerve to kiss me like you did, knowing all the while that you were planning to sue me?' she asked James, uncaring that shock and dismay had her exposing to public ridicule details of her private life that she normally wouldn't have shared with a single soul.

'I was,' James replied, pure rage smoking in his eyes, 'but that——'

'What took you so long to get around to telling me to my face, or does your gall stop short of that sort of straightforward decency?'

'You would have heard it from me if, in fact——'

'Save it!' she wailed, horribly afraid that she was going to burst into angry, hurt tears—in front of the whole of Port Armstrong, no less, because surely, by now, everyone must know that the best entertainment in town was happening live on the local TV station.

Don Hellerman rubbed his hands together gleefully. 'The little lady is upset.'

'Call me that one more time,' Melody promised, launching herself out of her chair with a speed that surprised even her, 'and I'll give new meaning to the term "lady" that will wipe the smirk off your face faster than you can possibly imagine!'

'Oh,' he chortled, as bedlam erupted in the audience, 'now we see the other side of this saintly front we've all been led to believe is so sincere.'

James was out of his chair, too. 'Shut up,' he snarled at the surprised host. 'Melody——'

'You shut up, too, James Logan!' she spat. 'Don't ever talk to me again!'

He said something more that was drowned out by the babble from the audience. He tried to cross the set to reach her, and managed to entangle himself in the nest of electrical wiring that snaked across the floor. She didn't wait for him to humiliate himself by falling flat on his face. Nothing he did could come close to matching the absolute fool she'd let him make of her. Beside him, Don Hellerman was a pathetic amateur, a sleazy, third-rate television performer whose opinions weren't worth a second thought.

Given her preference, she would have run out of the studio as fast as she could in her high-heeled boots, but pride forced her to stalk with regal disdain past the assembled corps of gaping stagehands and producers.

She didn't betray emotion by so much as a blink. She would have died before she would let any of them know that she was crying inside. She was crying not because she was hurt or angry or embarrassed—she'd been hurt and angry and embarrassed before and lived to talk about it—but because, underneath all that, something more serious had happened.

Some time between the night of Seth's accident and the day he had finally shown signs of recovering, she'd come close to falling in love with his arrogant, insulting, horrible son. But only now, when James had shown himself in his true colours, had she been shocked into realising what had happened. And she was crying because she'd seen the danger signs and ignored them, even though she was both old enough and smart enough to know better.

She soaked in the bath-tub for almost an hour, then lit a fire and made herself hot chocolate with marshmallows floating on the top, because they were all things that had comforted her in times of trouble for as far back as she could remember. From the CD player, Richard Clayderman spun romantic improvisations around classical piano favourites whose melodies she knew as well as her own name but whose titles she seldom could remember.

Content to immerse herself in the music and the fire's glow, she didn't light any lamps or candles. For a change, it was clear outside and a full moon rode above the trees. Across the lawn, ribbons of mist rose from the small creek that ran through the garden. It would have been a magical night, if things had been different.

Her chest hurt and she knew the only way to ease the pain was to let the tears come. Perversely, they wouldn't. She never could cry when she needed to, when it might have done some good, only when it meant giving in to weakness.

The intercom that alerted residents to callers at the main front door of the building buzzed loudly, an ugly counterpoint to the tranquillity she was trying so carefully to create. Since she neither expected nor wanted visitors, she ignored it, and eventually whoever it was went away again. The hot chocolate worked its old magic, and she snuggled down inside her velour robe, feeling almost relaxed. And then her peace was disturbed a second time.

'Open the door, Melody,' James ordered from the hall directly outside her apartment. 'I know you're there, and I'm not going away until you let me in.'

Drop dead, she thought balefully, and turned up the volume on the CD player. He'd get tired first. Her door was almost as thick as the main front door and could withstand anything James Logan had to offer in way of punishment.

'Me...lo...dy!' he bellowed, drowning out Richard Clayderman with no trouble at all.

The old lady who lived in the apartment above knocked on the floor in protest. Frustrated, Melody ground her teeth, turned down the volume of the music, and went to the door. 'Go away,' she said, sliding back the small oak panel which served as a peep-hole for checking out visitors. 'You're upsetting my neighbours.'

One blue eye smouldered on the other side. 'Let me in,' James roared, quite unmoved by the information, 'before you upset me!'

'I will not,' she retorted. 'And if you keep this up, I'll call the police and have you removed forcibly.'

'If intimidation's the name of the game,' James warned her, his tone no less moderate, 'you're going to have to come up with something more original than that.'

'Don't tempt me,' she replied. 'I learned first-hand this evening how to play dirty if I have to.' And she snapped the panel shut with a decisive little click.

The peace was almost as short-lived as her dubious satisfaction at having apparently had the last word. Without warning, James attacked the door, landing it a solid blow that had it shuddering on its hinges. 'Either you let me in, Melody,' he advised the whole building, clearly disinclined to lower his voice by so much as a decibel, 'or I'll say what I came to say out here in the hall, where your neighbours can hear every word. And I'll begin with the way you attacked me in the car that——'

'I'm calling the police, right now!'

He laughed, a smoky, sexy growl of amusement that, God help her, had her breaking out in goose-bumps. 'Honey, they won't come running for something like that. Kissing a man in the front seat of his car isn't a crime.' And, just to remind her that he was past all redemption, he grabbed the door-handle and gave it a wrench that had it creaking pitifully. 'Now open up and let me in.'

'Young man!' Melody heard her neighbour declare querulously from the landing upstairs. 'Young man, I am an old lady who needs her rest. Stop that racket this instant or I shall call the police, and I assure you that they will not hesitate to believe my version of your atrocious behaviour.'

This time, the silence lasted slightly longer, then, 'I beg your pardon, ma'am,' James replied soberly. 'I'm afraid I've been acting like a thoughtless fool.'

And to Melody's mingled relief and regret, his foot-steps faded away. Shortly after, she heard a car engine start up, saw the sweep of headlights flash briefly over her windows, and then there was nothing to disturb the peace of the night but Richard Clayderman playing *'Claire de Lune'*.

The next day was sheer hell.

'You were a disaster,' Roger greeted Melody the minute she set foot in Cat's Alley. 'Don Hellerman wiped the floor with you.'

'What else did you expect? Grown women who engage in make-believe and dressing-up aren't playing with a full deck,' Chloe said. 'It serves you right for sending a child to do a woman's job.'

'*Ma pauvre petite,*' Emile murmured, patting Melody's hand.

Ariadne eyed her with new respect. 'Did the handsome one really kiss you, Melody? It must have been...ahhh!' She kissed the tips of her fingers, flung them wide as if she were releasing a butterfly, and sighed blissfully. 'Words...they fail me.'

'Well, they don't fail me,' Chloe snapped. 'I hope you know, Melody Worth, that you're on your own with this lawsuit James Logan's threatening. I said from the beginning this whole charity affair would cause nothing but trouble and I was right. Let people learn to look out for themselves the hard way, as I've had to do.'

'God forbid we should all adopt your attitude,' Justin said. 'Melody, you think he really intends to go ahead with litigation? I thought his father was making a good recovery.'

Roger snorted in contempt. 'Justin, you ought to know better than anyone that recovery's only part of the picture. Even if the old man walks out of that hospital as good as new, he can claim damages for mental anguish and all that sort of stuff. The bottom line here is that if James Logan sues on his father's behalf we could all end up on the breadline. No judge within fifty miles is going to find in our favour, not after the sort of publicity we got yesterday. No offence, Melody, but you couldn't have made a worse mess of things if you'd tried. Why didn't you refute Hellerman's accusations, instead of spreading your love-life all over the front page?'

'A man having the nerve to try to kiss a woman does not, in my book, constitute a love-life,' Melody replied, chagrined all over again. 'And just for the record, Ariadne, the earth didn't move at the time.'

But her heart turned over just at the memory of James's lips brushing over hers. How had he managed to do so much damage in so short a time?

'You could have fooled us,' Chloe drawled in disgust. 'The way you behaved, I thought he must be the reincarnation of all the great Hollywood lovers rolled into one, and had proposed at the very least.'

'He was a damned fool if he didn't,' Justin said.

'And she'd be a bigger fool if she accepted,' Chloe shot back. 'Anyway, I take it marriage isn't on his mind since he's talking lawsuits, so let's get back to what really matters. Who's going to pay if he goes ahead?'

'I told you once before that if it came to that I'd take full responsibility,' Melody said wearily. The way she felt right then, she didn't care if she did end up bankrupt. No doubt Chloe had her reasons for being so uncompromisingly cynical about men in general, but James had destroyed enough of Melody's ideals for one week. She didn't feel up to stomaching any more disenchantment.

For the most part, she'd been very lucky with the men who'd figured romantically in her life. Although none had attracted her with the same compelling force that James Logan managed to exert, they had, without exception, been pleasant, civilised people who'd treated her with respect. The idea that someone of James's ob-

noxious arrogance might be the one to steal her heart
struck a most disquieting note.

If the number of people who later showed up in
Yesteryear 'just to look around' was any indication,
Chloe wasn't alone in her opinion. Some might call it
paranoia, but Melody felt certain that the chief interest
lay less in the classic clothing than in the classic fool
who collected it. The curiosity of the customers burned
holes in her from all sides. She was glad when it was
time to shut up shop for the day.

'I'd consult a lawyer if I were you,' Roger said,
catching up with her as she left Cat's Alley. 'We all know
that Chloe can be a real bitch at times, but in this case
she's right. If Logan sues, it could cost you everything.'

Good advice, Melody knew, and she supposed she had
an obligation to be prepared to defend herself, if only
because James did not deserve an easy victory. So she
paid a visit to her friend and legal adviser, Will McAllister
and, as a result, arrived home at seven o'clock, instead
of her customary six.

It had been a beautiful day, clear and windless. The
waters over the Strait had shone with the same deep,
calm blue they wore in summer, and the first snowdrops
were opening in sheltered parts of the gardens. By the
time Melody climbed the steps to the front door of
Stonehouse Mansion, however, the moon had risen and
diamond points of frost glistened on the drive.

Once inside her own front door, she dumped her boots,
coat and bag in the entrance hall and, unbuttoning her
blouse as she went, trailed into her bedroom. It was
another night for fleecy robes, furry slippers, a fire, and
nourishment that soothed the spirit as well as the
stomach—in that order.

A small brass lamp on the desk near the living-room
door was all the light she needed to see her way to the

hearth. She always kept a supply of seasoned cherry wood and kindling handy, and in no time at all she had a fire roaring up the chimney.

'I'm impressed,' a voice proclaimed from the depths of the armchair behind her.

A yelp of shock about an octave higher than her usual tone escaped Melody before she could smother it, but the fear that momentarily choked her quickly evaporated into weary resignation. 'Why?' she asked. 'Because I don't have elves hidden under the floorboards who pop out and do menial chores for me when I'm not home? Or because I haven't fainted dead away at the unwelcome sound of your voice?'

'A little bit of both,' James said, unfolding from the chair to tower over her, 'though, now that you mention it, I admit the second reason appeals more to my vanity.'

'Sorry to disappoint you, then,' Melody said, tying the belt of her robe more tightly around her waist as though by doing so she could ward off evil spirits. 'I guess I'm made of sterner stuff than you realised.'

'Either that,' James observed thoughtfully, 'or you're used to coming home to find men lounging about in your living-room. Which is it, Melody?'

'None of your business.'

He took a step closer. 'That's about as innovative a reply as "I'll call the cops if you don't go away."'

'I never used the word "cops". It's vulgar.'

He beamed with pure delight, his dimples winking in the firelight. 'I can be a very vulgar man on occasion, my lady, believe me.'

'Oh, I do,' she replied, a good deal more airily than she felt. Wasn't it enough that his teeth were spectacularly perfect, without his having been blessed with dimples, too? 'I have no trouble believing that at all.'

'I didn't come here to fight, Melody.'

'I don't care why you came. All that matters to me is that you leave, the sooner the better.'

He shook his head. 'No way, darling. Not until you and I have had a little talk.'

'There's a telephone on the table over there, and all it takes——'

'Is one call to the cops...' He sighed with exaggerated patience, and proclaimed in a ludicrous falsetto, '"Help, officer! There's a strange man in my room!"'

Melody tried not to smile. 'Are you admitting you're strange, James?' she enquired sweetly, edging towards the phone.

'Forget it, Melody,' he warned in his normal tone. 'You don't stand a chance of making that call.'

She was faintly disgusted to discover that the thought of his stopping her caused a wave of excitement to flow through her. 'I could scream,' she suggested. 'Then my neighbour upstairs would do the calling for me.'

This time, his smile caressed her with appalling familiarity, settling at the point where the neck of her robe dipped open above her breasts. 'She's not home. I saw her leave in a taxi just after I climbed up on to your balcony. You shouldn't leave your spare key in such an obvious place, darling. You never know who might find it.'

'What exactly do you want, James?' Melody enquired wrathfully, since he obviously had her cornered.

'To talk.'

'Well, say your piece. I'm hungry, and I'd like to eat dinner before morning.'

'We can eat and talk at the same time.'

'You misunderstood. I wasn't inviting you to dinner. I wasn't expecting company,' she informed him, forestalling the objections with which she knew he would override that statement, 'and I don't have anything to offer you.'

'That's OK. We can send out for something. How about pizza?'

'I don't like pizza.'

'Too simple for your expensive tastes, no doubt. How about Japanese?'

'I was planning to have beans.'

For a change, he was the one caught by surprise. 'Beans?' he echoed. 'You mean . . . ?'

'Baked beans, on toast.'

He recovered quickly. 'I like beans,' he said, with a winsome smile.

'Who first said, "If you can't beat 'em, join 'em"?' Melody wondered aloud, and shrugged in defeat. 'You open the beans, and I'll make the toast,' she said and swept towards the kitchen, noting with peripheral satisfaction that he kept a sharp eye on the phone as she passed it by.

She had the bread sliced for toast and was preparing the hot chocolate when she realised that James was not having much success opening the can of beans. 'Are all left-handed people as awkward as you?' she asked, as the opener slipped for the third time and the can went rolling on the floor.

'I'm not left-handed,' he muttered, and flexed the fingers on his right hand tenderly.

'James!' Dismayed, Melody noticed the bruised and broken skin over his swollen knuckles. 'What happened to you?'

'Would you believe I punched your door too hard last night?'

'No,' she said, pressing a lever on her refrigerator to release crushed ice into a bowl. 'You didn't do this much damage from banging on my door. What aren't you telling me?'

'I lost my temper.' He looked at her from under his silky black lashes. 'I punched someone out.'

'Good lord! Look at the mess you made of your hand.'

His expression hung midway between a smirk of satisfaction and a grimace of pain. 'You should see the other guy.'

'Who was he?' she demanded, taking his hand and submerging it into the crushed ice.

'That's cold,' he said.

He was standing awfully close. She supposed it was unavoidable, in the circumstances, so why was she shaking? It wasn't as if he were crowding her, or anything. 'Stop complaining and answer the question.'

'Don Hellerman.'

Melody's mouth fell open. 'The TV host?'

'The very same. In fact,' James teased her, 'his jaw fell about as far as yours just did—but a lot harder.' He flexed his fingers again. 'I'd have hit him a second time if his flunkies hadn't rescued him.'

'Violence,' Melody said primly, 'seldom accomplishes any good. You ought to know better.'

'Maybe not in your kind of world, my lady,' James replied, cradling his swollen fingers in his other hand, 'but where I grew up, it settled a lot of disagreements, and although I don't normally advocate its use there are times when a punch in the mouth is a hell of lot cleaner and more up front than the so-called civilised methods you might employ.'

She shoved his injured fingers back into the bowl of ice. 'You could be charged with assault.'

'I was provoked.'

'You'll wind up spending more time in court than at your father's bedside at this rate.'

Once again, he removed his hand from the ice pack, and this time he removed the bowl, too, and emptied its contents into the sink. 'That's one of the things I want to talk to you about.'

She wished she'd kept her mouth shut. She didn't want to be reminded of the reasons she had for being furious with him, for despising him, for having every reason in the world to throw him out of her apartment. 'Talk to my lawyer,' she said stiffly, turning away to tend to the toast, which had grown cold.

He moved around the counter and came to stand so close behind her that her whole body vibrated with awareness. 'Melody.'

'What?'

'Look at me.' He took her by the shoulders and spun her around, and when she still refused to meet his gaze he grasped her chin and tilted her face up to his. 'I'm sorry I hurt you,' he said.

She tried to toss off a little smile, one that was supposed to tell him it would take more than anything he could come up with to hurt her. But it faltered, and, even though he still held it gently between his thumb and forefinger, she felt her chin begin to wobble dangerously. The smart thing would have been to cut her losses while she could, but she seemed to have lost all power of smart thinking practically from the day he'd barged into her life.

'I don't know what you're talking about,' she quavered, in a disgustingly pathetic little voice.

James uttered a sigh similar to the one he'd allowed himself shortly before he'd kissed her the first time, that day in his car. It was a sigh full of baffled frustration, as though he didn't know how in the world he'd managed to turn a simple mission of mercy to his ailing father into so complicated and dangerous an undertaking. Then he moved closer, so that her hips were pinned against the kitchen cabinets. Even if her brain had been in charge, she couldn't have obeyed it and moved out of the danger zone. He had her trapped.

CHAPTER SIX

'I ADMIT,' James said, taking shameless advantage of the fact that she was a captive audience, 'that I think you're misguided in assuming you know what's best for people you don't begin to understand. I also admit that my first intention when I heard about Seth's accident was to sue you and anyone else connected with that insane fund-raising event. But that was then, before...' He stopped, wetted his lips, and gave her a tiny shake. 'Stop looking at me like that, Melody, before I do something I'll live to regret.'

She couldn't help herself. His voice was a low and lazy rumble and, instead of paying attention to what he was saying, she stared at his mouth, hypnotised by the shapes it assumed as he spoke. There was really only one word to describe James Logan, and it wasn't 'obnoxious' or 'arrogant' or 'despicable', as she'd tried telling herself. The word was 'sexy'.

Everything he did, and just about everything he said, was sexy. And the wonder of it—or should it be the danger?—was that he either didn't know, or didn't care. He was so busy being careful not to get too entangled with her that he was oblivious to the effect he had on her.

And that, she was forced to admit, was that the more she saw of him, and the longer she knew him, the more enmeshed she became in the web of his charm. He wasn't the kind of man she'd envisaged falling in love with. He wasn't the kind of man she'd expected she might some day marry. He didn't fit any of the roles she'd thought might suit her. Yet despite all that, plus the fact that he sometimes made her so angry that she could spit nails, he was the only man who intrigued and challenged her to the point that she feared it might take all of this life, and a good portion of the hereafter, before she was likely to run the risk of growing bored with him.

'What might you do, James?' she asked him softly.

His thumbs slid down her throat and inside her robe. They searched out her collarbones and explored the line of her shoulders. He pulled her against him, held her so close that she had no doubt at all about what he wanted to do that he'd live to regret, and she felt an answering surge of desire inside herself that startled her. She fluttered her eyes closed quickly, before they relayed the information to him.

'I might kiss you,' he threatened, his voice abrasive against her mouth, 'and then I just might ravish you, here on the kitchen floor.'

Shocked less by what he said than by the anger underlying his words, her eyes flew wide. 'Not on the floor!'

'Then open the damned can of beans and stop playing games.'

Games? She had never been more serious in her life! 'I wasn't,' she protested.

He moved away, leaving a chill to take the place of his warmth. 'Yes, you were. You were playing grand lady toying with the passions of the village lout. Well, you don't need to bother. I've already told you, I don't plan to sue. If you'd stayed and heard me out yesterday, instead of running off in a snit, I'd have told you then, with half the residents of this trendy little town as witnesses. And then that sleazy Hellerman might have kept his big mouth shut long enough for me to make it out of that benighted television studio without feeling a need to deck him.'

'So it's all my fault that you can't control yourself?'

He sighed heavily again. 'My dear lady, if that was the only complaint I had against you I'd offer to take you out to dinner. As it is, I think the sanest move is for me to take myself out of your kitchen fast, and leave you to enjoy your baked beans on toast alone.'

Not for the world would she let him see how badly she wanted him to stay. 'Good,' she said loftily. 'There isn't enough for two, anyway.'

'And you probably aren't used to having to share,' he shot back.

He left by the front door, covered the distance to his car in seconds flat, slammed it into gear, and shot off down the drive before he changed his mind.

He couldn't believe he'd nearly done it again. Another minute, another breath, and he'd have kissed her. And if she'd thought he was joking when he'd said he'd have made love to her there on the kitchen floor, then she didn't know a desperate man when she saw one, and shouldn't be allowed out alone.

Not 'made love', he corrected himself. Had sex. That was all it would have been. Hell, he'd have to be six feet under not to have become aroused by the sight of her in her clinging little robe that kept gaping open just enough to whet his appetite then sliding closed again before he had the chance to satisfy it.

Lucky for her that she kept her wine rack where she did. His restraint had more to do with his having spotted the rows of expensive champagne than it had with chivalry. He was quite sure that, if he'd looked, he'd have found a couple of bottles chilling in her refrigerator. And probably a couple of cases stashed in one of the cupboards, just in case she found she needed them in a hurry.

She'd probably have laughed if he'd told her of the memory resurrected by the sight of those elegant green bottles with their gold collars. He'd recalled the time she'd told him she'd bathe in champagne, given the choice. It had been a timely reminder that she and he came from separate worlds.

Never mind that he'd made something different of his life and mixed with high society now. It didn't alter the fact that she had a pedigree a mile long. He'd seen enough to know that plain old red blood didn't mix well with aristocratic blue, starting with the day he'd turned twelve and got his first Saturday job as a delivery boy for one of the town grocers. 'Don't you know better than to come to the front door?' the lady of the house had asked, with a pained expression on her face. 'Use the service entrance the next time.'

He switched on the radio, then snapped it off again in a hurry as he recognised the song being played. 'Angel Eyes' might have been written for Melody Worth. In fact, eyes like hers ought to be outlawed. They made him want to sink into their soft velvet depths, and that was enough to make his mind and body stray to other lustful urgings.

Doggedly, he tuned his thoughts to more productive channels. How, for example, was he going to deal with Seth in the coming weeks? The good news was that his father was going to be released from the hospital. The bad news was that he needed full-time out-patient care for another month at least, or until such time as he could manage to look after himself. And that wasn't going to happen until he became accustomed to getting about on crutches.

There were other options. First, Seth could use a wheelchair. Second, he could allow a professional home-help to visit every day for a few weeks. But, being Seth, he was resisting the first suggestion and had flatly vetoed the second, leaving James with little choice but to extend his stay in town. Worse, he was going to have to move into his father's house, which should make for some pretty heated exchanges. They couldn't spend five minutes in the same room without falling out, so God only knew what it would be like living under the same roof together.

Melody would know how to coax Seth into sense. All she'd have to do was appeal to him with those great, innocent eyes of hers and...

James scowled, and took a corner too fast, forgetting that a slick of black ice covered the road. The car swung gracefully around and came to a halt with its nose pointing back the way he'd just come.

The blasted vehicle had more sense than he had! Why had he accused her of playing games when a fool could have seen that she was utterly sincere? For the sadistic pleasure of punishing her—or himself? Oh, she'd done a good job of covering up, had flung his rejection back in his face with her usual fire. But not quite soon enough for him to have missed the hurt that turned her eyes into bottomless pools. Not quite soon enough to hide the sudden unhappy droop to her sweet, soft mouth.

He swore, and slammed his fist against the steering-wheel. He flinched as the pain shot through his fingers all the way up to his elbow, and swore again, with fluent vulgarity.

He wasn't the kind of guy who kicked puppies and children. He didn't go out of his way to hurt other people's feelings just to make himself feel better. He liked to think that, working-class origins notwithstanding, there was a bit of the white knight in him somewhere, a basic decency that compelled him to rescue old ladies from burning buildings, and allowed him to deal kindly with the occasional woman who became too persistent with her demands on his affections. When had he changed?

He knew when. It was the day he'd come back to Port Armstrong and been caught in the crossfire between its different segments of society. Damn this miserable little town and everyone in it!

Melody made fresh toast, opened the can of beans, placed them to heat in the microwave oven, and filled the Thermos with hot chocolate. When everything was ready, she carried it on a tray to the living-room, and settled herself on the rug in front of the fire.

No music tonight, she decided. She wasn't in the mood. Not that she was sad, she insisted, blinking furiously at the flames, so there was no reason to start crying. It wasn't as if she'd lost anything; she'd merely fooled herself into thinking she'd found something, and James had disabused her of that notion before it had had time to take proper root.

A slight thud outside the French doors made her look up. Something tapped against one of the panes, and James's face appeared. 'Hi,' he mouthed, and smiled with a sort of lop-sided uncertainty, as if he feared he might end up wearing the beans she was about to eat.

She didn't have the energy to go through a repeat of last night's fiasco. It was easier just to let him in, hear him out, and get it over with—always assuming he had anything he wished to say. More likely, he'd left a coat behind, or something. All he was wearing to protect him from the cold were black cords and his heavy fisherman's-knit sweater over a pale grey cotton shirt.

She opened the door and indicated with a nod that he could come inside. Then she backed away, folded her hands, and waited.

'I'm sorry,' he said, stalking her to the fireplace. 'I'm a miserable, insensitive clod—but only when I'm around you.'

'Is that supposed to make me feel better, James?'

'No,' he allowed, 'but it makes me feel better. I'd hate to think I couldn't find an excuse for behaving the way I did.'

He looked at her, waiting for her to say something. She searched for a suitable response—something gracious, perhaps, to let him know that she was a perfect lady, or something cutting, because he deserved it. She waved a hand at the tray. 'Do you want some beans?'

One dimple appeared. 'Sure.'

'I'll get an extra plate and——'

He restrained her by catching the tail-end of her belt as she made to pass by him. 'Let me.'

While he rattled drawers and opened cupboards, she replenished the fire. He came back, shucked off his sweater, and sank down beside her on the rug. In doing so, he pulled his shirt-tail loose from his trousers, which might have looked slightly ridiculous on any other man but which merely enhanced his already potent masculine appeal.

'You make me crazy, you know,' he said, scooping half her beans on to his plate and snitching a slice of toast. 'I had a nice, orderly life until you came along and messed things up.'

'That's a totally unjust accusation,' she said without much conviction, because she knew exactly what he meant. The mere fact of his existence was all it took to turn her world upside-down.

'I realise,' he said, chewing meditatively on a piece of toast, 'that a person can do only so much to control his fate, and that it's the unexpected that makes life interesting. I mean, heaven forbid every day should be the same.'

'Heaven forbid,' she echoed faintly, fascinated all over again by the sexy way he moved his mouth when he spoke.

'On the other hand, only a fool insists on trying to reshape his life to fit a mould that was never designed to accommodate it.'

She nodded. 'Square pegs.'

'And round holes. Exactly! Take you and me, for instance.' He threw a glance at her, and looked away again rather hurriedly. 'I'm a naval architect, which makes me more of a mathematician than an artist. Although I do have an eye for good lines, I design ships primarily for speed and safety. And you . . .' He paused.

'I collect old clothes,' Melody supplied for him, remembering Chloe's comment about a grown woman making a career out of playing dressing-up. 'What are you getting at, James?'

He put down his plate with a clatter. His profile, etched by the fire's glow, was disturbingly handsome. 'Background and upbringing apart, we're incompatible,' he said.

She didn't know what came over her. 'I know,' she said, and slid her hand up under his shirt to caress his chest. She knew already that he was a big man, but it wasn't the width of his chest, the muscle that underlay the firm, smooth flesh, the bone that held the frame together, that impressed her. It was the power they signified—a strength of the mind, of the spirit—which would endure no matter how time or circumstance might ravage his body.

She'd taken him by surprise. She felt his heart miss a beat, then try to make up for it by racing erratically. She

felt a sudden heat permeate his skin, felt an answering
warmth flow within herself.

Very slowly, he turned to look at her. He examined
her jaw, her cheekbones, her hair. Reluctantly, he stared
into her eyes, and closed his own briefly. His fingers
covered hers, and for a moment she thought he was going
to remove her hand. Then he looked at her mouth and,
instead of pushing her away, he drew her forward until
his lips grazed hers.

He started to say something and she knew that if she
allowed the words to emerge the spell would be broken.
He would express reservations and doubts and, once they
were out in the open, the long-term consequences would
be all that mattered.

She didn't care about any of it. It wasn't tomorrow,
or next year, that counted; it was this moment. It was
a primal instinct within herself that refused to be fet-
tered by anything as mundane as reason or logic. It was
being brave enough to listen to the urgings of a body
that was far more in tune than her mind with the true
state of her emotions.

She could heed those emotions and know that,
whatever the cost, she had had the courage to face the
truth. Or she could follow the conventionally correct
objections thrown up by her conscience, which opted
for safety and propriety. Was she going to take the easy
way out—she, who'd appeared before the whole town
on public television and taken a stand on what she believed in? Not likely!

So she slid her other hand around his neck and sealed
her mouth to his. She put her whole soul into that kiss
in an effort to melt his resistance quickly, before she lost
her nerve.

She succeeded faster and better than she could ever
have hoped because he kissed her back, not gently or

reluctantly at all, but with immediate fire and passion. His hands skimmed over her, pulled her hard against him. The silky velour of her robe slipped aside. The fire was warm on her exposed thigh, nearly as warm as his lips against hers.

The room tilted as the rug came up to cushion her head. James hovered above her, uncovering her, touching her, watching her. She saw her own hands undo each button on his shirt, saw them slide over his naked shoulders and trail down to the wash-board hardness of his stomach.

'If you just want to prove that you can drive me mad,' he warned her softly, his voice not quite a growl but too feral to qualify as a purr, 'consider the experiment a success. But if that's all you want...' his hand stopped, just short of the elasticised lace band that held up her panties '... then call a halt now, because if you wait any longer it will be too late.'

'If you stop now,' she managed to whisper past the ache in her throat, 'I'll die.'

The words didn't strike her as at all melodramatic or silly. It was the only way she knew how to tell him that she needed him to make love to her more than she needed to breathe.

His hand shaped her waist, slid down to banish her underwear until she was completely naked. He brushed his lips down her neck and brought them to rest on the swollen peak of one breast. His fingers traced forbidden paths down her ribs and over her hips, found her, awoke her. Warmth turned to heat, and she dissolved into indecent pleasure.

'Please...' she whispered, needing more.

A simple enough plea, perhaps, but her hunger infected him, inflamed him, just as it tormented her. Silk joined corduroy in a careless heap. Velour slithered away to nest over discarded shoes. One eighteen-carat gold hoop earring snagged in her hair, and she reached up to free it and tossed it away as blithely as if it were brass.

She clung to him, marvelling at the texture of him, the scent of him, the taste of him. And when he tried to slow her down, she wrapped her legs around his waist and shamelessly captured him.

He tensed; he groaned. She thought he cursed, softly, helplessly. Then he slipped both hands beneath her and made her as securely his prisoner as she'd made him hers. With awesome determination, he wrenched desire into submission just long enough to teach her that she wasn't the only one who could drive a person to the brink of insanity.

And then the tempo changed, the pace and mood governed not by anything that each of them could offer separately, but by what they created and shared together. It was terrifying and it was magnificent, and all too brief. She thought the detonation would destroy them both.

He lifted his head a long time later and looked down at her. His hair clung damply to his forehead, the ends curling slightly. 'I ravished you on the floor after all,' he said, with the glimmer of a smile.

She sighed dreamily. 'But not in the kitchen!'

It wasn't what she wanted to say at all. She wanted to tell him that he could protest all he liked about their not being compatible, but that she knew differently. She wanted to have him carry her to the bedroom and hold her in his arms for the rest of the night. But most of all, she wanted to tell him she loved him.

'It's getting late,' she said quickly, before she did untold damage.

He rolled away and pushed himself into a sitting position. 'Right.'

What did two people say to each other while they disentangled their clothing and covered themselves up? It was ridiculous to feel embarrassed about his seeing her with nothing on when she'd just shared with him the ultimate intimacy. Yet the silence hung between them, fraught with tension. She couldn't stand it.

'Seth seemed to be doing well when I last visited him,' she said, scooting inside her robe.

'He is,' James replied, climbing into his clothes with equally unflattering haste. 'So well, in fact, that they're sending him home in a couple of days.'

Cold dread clutched her heart. 'Does that mean you'll be leaving town, James?'

He looked up from buckling his belt. 'Sooner or later, yes.'

She couldn't help it. 'When?' she asked, on a frail breath.

'What does it matter?' he replied evenly. 'You've known all along that I wouldn't be staying. Or has something happened to make you believe differently?'

It was a direct challenge. A braver woman would have accepted it and risked everything, but Melody found she wasn't nearly as full of courage now as she had been an hour ago. 'Not a thing,' she said. 'You have your own life to get back to—we both know that—and I suppose you might as well get on with it right away.'

'Not quite that soon,' he said, tugging his sweater into place and combing his hair with his fingers. 'It'll take a week or two to get Seth settled at the house. He's being difficult, as usual, and refusing to accept the help available to him, so he's stuck with me as his nursemaid.'

Oh, she loved Seth almost as much as she loved his son! 'Well,' she said, walking James to the door, 'let me know if there's anything I can do to help.'

'Try to convince him to co-operate.'

'Of course. I'll go and see him before he's discharged.'

'Thanks.'

Another awkward pause she rushed to fill. 'Goodnight, then.'

'Goodnight.' He stopped just outside the apartment and threw her a hunted look. 'Melody, about tonight——'

An awful sense of foreboding gripped her. He was going to humiliate her by apologising, or by saying what a ghastly mistake they'd just made. She could think of nothing worse.

'Don't go making something out of nothing,' pride had her saying. 'We got carried away, I know, and we probably shouldn't have, but we don't have to spoil a pleasant interlude with reproaches or warnings. You're under no obligations to me, James, nor I to you. Let's just leave it at that.'

'Still friends?' he enquired, holding out his hand.

She'd been wrong. There *was* something worse than an apology. 'Of course,' she said, almost gagging on the reply.

She didn't take his outstretched hand. Instead, she lifted hers in farewell and closed the door. She heard his footsteps recede down the hall, heard the Mansion's heavy front door thud closed behind him. With the utmost composure, she listened to the sound of his car drive away. Then she sat down on the floor, right where he'd left her, and burst into tears.

What a silly fool she was! She'd believed that only the moment mattered, and had found out too late that one moment could alter the rest of time, because she knew now that nothing would ever be the same for her again. Nothing would seem right without James there to share it with her.

*   *   *

Seth glared from his wheelchair by the window. 'They're looking to kill me, one way or another,' he informed Melody when she stopped in for her promised visit the day before he was sent home from the hospital. 'They haven't managed to do it here, so they're springing me loose and leaving the job to someone else.'

'You surely don't mean your son?' Melody folded Seth's few possessions into the new canvas tote bag that James had dropped off that morning, and fought the adolescent urge to hug the bag against her heart. It was bad enough that she twisted the conversation in any way she could in order to mention James's name, without going over the edge about him.

One thing she could be sure of was that he wasn't pining for the sight or sound of her. Obviously he'd decided that the better part of discretion lay in visiting his father when he knew she was tied to the shop.

She checked the drawers and locker one last time. 'He's not going to kill you, Seth, unless he's a really lousy cook.'

'I'm not talking about James.' Seth shook an impotent fist. 'I mean that busybody. That Nosy Parker. She'll be dropping in any old time she feels like it and minding my business for me.'

'Ah! You mean your caseworker.'

'Only case she belongs in is a suitcase lined with lead and dropped off the end of the dock.'

Despite her unhappiness, Melody had to smile. 'Have you met her already?'

Seth nodded. 'Smiles all the time,' he muttered gloomily. 'Has little curls that bob all over the place every time she nods her head. Looks like a bird hopping around waiting for the worm to surface—namely, me.'

'Don't be so hard on her. She sounds rather sweet.'

'Yeah,' he agreed derisively, massaging his knee, 'she's a real pistol all right.'

'She's just doing her job.'

'Let her do it on someone else. I don't need her.' He swung the wheelchair around, crashed into the end of the bed, and let out a howl of pain. 'Are you just goin' to stand there and watch a man suffer, girl? Help me get this dad-blamed machine set straight!'

'If you're so determined to be independent, Seth, you'd better start now,' Melody said, and went back to packing the bag.

'Ain't nothing colder than a woman's heart,' Seth mourned in a hollow voice. 'Reckon it would've been kinder if that big fancy car had backed up and finished me off, if this is the sort of sympathy I can look forward to.'

Melody bit her lip and resisted the impulse to run over and help him out. It was only because of exposure to Justin that she knew differently. He'd been the one to coach her on what to expect when he'd heard that Seth would be immobilised in a wheelchair for the first little while after he was discharged.

'Make him hate it enough to want to get out of it,' he advised. 'Start pushing him around in it and he'll push you around for the next year or more. He's got to work for his independence.'

'You might as well start now learning to manage without me, Seth,' she said. 'I'm not going to be around to help you when you get home.'

'Reckon now that you think I might mend, you don't have to be nice to me. Reckon now that they've given me a nursemaid, you won't want to bother to visit me, either.' He flung her an aggrieved glare. 'Reckon I liked you better when you thought I was dyin'.'

A pang of compassion made her blurt out the truth. 'I don't think James wants me visiting you, Seth. If it were up to me, I'd be over to see you every chance I got.'

'Don't want you feeling obligated,' he informed her, his gravelly old voice breaking. 'Don't need anyone feeling sorry for me.'

Once upon a time, Melody would have reacted differently to the accusation, but that was before she'd learned, first-hand, what loneliness was all about. She knew now that it had nothing to do with how many people surrounded a person. It had to do with an emptiness inside that only one in particular could fill. So, instead of scoffing at Seth for wallowing in self-pity, she went over and hugged him.

'I don't feel sorry for you,' she said. 'I'm too busy feeling sorry for myself.'

His gaze sharpened. 'That damned boy of mine giving you grief, Melody, girl?'

She shrugged. 'We give each other grief, I'm afraid.'

'Aye, well, that may be, but, as far as who comes to my house and who stays away, that's my choice, not James's, and I choose to have you paying calls whenever you feel like it. And I'll tell him I said so.'

'No, don't do that, Seth!' She could imagine how James would greet the news that she'd been complaining about him to his father. 'He didn't come right out and tell me to stay away. I just got the impression that I'd... well, be intruding on family time, that's all.'

'I'll set him straight on that, too,' Seth declared.

The next afternoon, James phoned her at the shop. 'I just struck a bargain with Seth,' he said. 'He'll allow his caseworker to visit if I'll let you in the door too. What puzzles me is why he thinks I'd turn you away. Did I ever say that?'

'Not exactly,' Melody said, hot flushes racing over her at the sound of his voice.

'I thought we'd agreed we're still friends, Melody.'

'We are.'

'Then what's the problem?'

I'm in love with you, and that puts a whole different complexion on things! 'I guess there isn't one.'

'Good,' he said briskly. 'Then how about coming over when you close up? Work some of your soothing magic on him. He came home this morning and nothing I've done to try to make him comfortable is working. If he's to be believed, I'm as irritating as a flea.'

A woman of intelligence would have balked at being used. A woman of spirit and determination would have resisted James Logan's sexy rumble of a voice.

'I'll be there around six,' Melody said, and spent her lunch-hour buying little delicacies to tempt the invalid's appetite.

CHAPTER SEVEN

MELODY drove up to Seth's house just as James was unloading groceries from his car. 'Here, let me give you a hand with that,' he said, relieving her of the oversized pink azalea she retrieved from her passenger seat, 'and I'll get the rest of the stuff later.'

A picket fence that might once have been painted white but which had long since been stripped to bare wood from exposure to the weather surrounded the small plot of land that was Seth's garden. Pushing aside a gate hanging creakily askew on its hinges, James led the way along a path that bisected a patch of coarse grass.

'Seth?' he called, shouldering open an even squeakier front door which led directly into the living-room.

Seth sat in a wheelchair, next to an open fireplace. 'What did you bring that dried-up old bush for?' he grumbled, scowling at the plant.

James stepped aside to reveal Melody behind him. 'I didn't. Melody did.'

Sly glee filled the old man's eyes. 'Most beautiful flower I ever saw!' he announced. 'Put it over here where I can see it.'

James made a wry face at her. 'See what I mean? I can't win no matter how hard I try.'

'Just come in and shut the door before I catch my death of cold,' Seth ordered. 'Melody, sit here on the sofa, next to the fire, and warm yourself.'

'I have a few more things in my car,' she said, trying not to stare at her surroundings. The interior of the little house was spotlessly clean and tidy, and about as cheerless as a prison cell. The furniture was basic, to say the least: the lumpy old sofa to which Seth had referred, a wooden table covered with oilcloth, two press-back chairs, a floor lamp and, in an arched alcove beyond, a sink, hotplate and ancient refrigerator. In one corner of the living area stood a small television; in the other, a staircase led up to a second floor that was probably no better than the rest of the cottage. Another door, facing the front entrance, stood ajar, revealing the foot of a single bed.

Not a picture or photograph graced the walls. Apart from the azalea, the only other adornment to be seen was a bedraggled tinsel garland tacked over the mantelpiece. It struck such a desolate, lonely note that Melody could hardly bear to look at it. She didn't want to know how Seth had coped with Christmas, a time meant for sharing with family.

'Let me have your car keys and I'll unload the things you want brought in,' James said.

She shook her head. 'I can get them myself.'

'No need. I have to bring in the rest of the supplies I brought, and I'm sure Seth would rather you spent the time visiting him—unless, of course, you don't want me going through your car.'

That was exactly what she didn't want! She could imagine the scorn with which he'd view her selection of treats for his father. Pheasant in aspic and lobster mayonnaise, imported Swedish cloudberry jelly and French pâté, to name a few, were about as suitable a choice as hemlock, given the circumstances.

James fixed her with an enquiring stare. 'Why the horrified face? Have you got a body stashed in the back seat, or something?'

'Don't be silly.' She managed a feeble laugh and handed over her keys. It was too late now to pretend all she'd brought with her was the plant. 'Anyway, I don't have a back seat.'

He was gone only a few minutes. She heard the gate creak in protest and then the front door was shoved open again. With both arms full of paper grocery bags and a pink and grey wicker basket hanging from one hand, James strode into the cottage.

'What you got there?' Seth wanted to know.

James spilled the contents of the bags over the table. 'Supplies,' he said tersely. 'Canned soups and stews, packages of macaroni and cheese, crackers, sliced bread, cheese, milk, coffee. Then there's this.' He indicated the basket with its silver-grey monogrammed lid, and read the attached label. '"Selections from Gourmet Elite, Port Armstrong's finest delicatessen". You probably have to have a degree in languages to pronounce the names of half the stuff.'

'Open it,' Seth ordered. 'I want to see what's inside.'

'Just your average, upper-class grocery items, I expect,' James sneered. 'Pickled quails' eggs and *escargots*, crystallised——'

Seth wheeled himself over to the table. 'What sort of cargo?'

'Snails.' James laughed, a nasty grating noise that set Melody's teeth on edge.

'There are no *escargots*,' she said.

Seth backed the chair away a good deal faster than he'd rolled it forward. 'There'd better not be! I might not be a millionaire, but I'm not reduced to eating garden slugs. What were you thinking of, Melody, girl?'

'She wasn't,' James explained with dripping sarcasm. 'She was acting out of habit and instinct.'

Melody marched over to the table and wrenched the basket away from him. 'Don't listen to your son, Seth. I chose these things very carefully because I thought you deserved something special to celebrate your home-coming. I'll describe everything that's here, and if there's something you don't think you want to try just tell me and I'll take it away again.'

'I don't know,' Seth muttered doubtfully. 'I don't like to appear ungrateful, but...'

'You won't hurt my feelings,' she promised and picked up the pâté. 'This is meat paste. You can spread it on bread or crackers.' She hauled out the cloudberry jelly. 'And this is fruit jam from Scandinavia. It tastes wonderful on——'

'Croissants from Paris,' James interjected scornfully. 'But gee, guess what? The corner store didn't happen to have any fresh ones on hand.'

She glared at him. 'How thoughtless of them! Fortunately, toast will do just as well.'

'Don't sound all that bad to me,' Seth admitted, chancing another glance into the hamper. 'Show me what else you've got.'

'Pheasant, which is a lot like chicken, and cooked lobster. They're both ready to eat, so you don't have to go to any trouble preparing them. Then there's, let me see...eggnog, and apricot tarts. A little smoked salmon. Nothing very extraordinary, really.'

'What, no nightingales' tongues?' James taunted, tight-lipped with displeasure.

'Quiet, boy, before you put me off my feed!' Seth ordered, rummaging through the basket like a child with a Christmas stocking, and waving the last item in the air. 'What's this, Melody?'

'*Babas au rhum*,' she informed him, refusing to acknowledge James's snort of contempt.

'Rum?' Seth grinned. 'I'm not sure what the baba part is all about, girl, but rum's always good for what ails a man!'

James muttered something unflattering and disappeared into the alcove to put away the supplies he'd bought, making a great deal of noise as he did so. Acutely uncomfortable, Melody sat and chatted with Seth a few minutes longer, then rose to leave.

'I don't want to overtire you on your first day home, but I'll stay longer the next time,' she promised, mentally adding, When you'll hopefully be alone! 'Actually, Seth, I'd like to talk to you about the plans to convert the old fish cannery to a community centre. I know that you weren't very pleased when you realised I was involved in the project, but I still don't understand why you're so opposed to it.'

James poked his head out of the kitchen. 'Because I spelled out for him what you wanted to do as I understand it.'

'Then it's no wonder he's so sceptical,' Melody replied tartly, and turned her back on him. 'You might have noticed, Seth, that your son's greatest pleasure comes from offering criticism.'

'There's something wrong with a project if it can't survive a little criticism,' James informed the room at large.

'There's something wrong with a person who can't see his way clear to a more positive approach,' Melody said to Seth, who snickered with evil enjoyment at the battle he was witnessing. 'That's the sort of negative input we don't need.'

A cast-iron frying-pan hit the stove with unnecessary force. 'Maybe,' James declared, 'there's no need for any input at all. Maybe the people whose lives you're so hell-bent on changing want things left just the way they are.'

'Could be he's right for once,' Seth said, regarding her from under shaggy brows.

Melody looked around at the bare necessities that comprised his home, and wanted to ask, How can you say that when what we're proposing can only improve the quality of your life? But James's words came back to haunt her. 'They don't want your charity. They resent it. Furthermore, it does nothing to solve the underlying problems.'

She looked back at Seth, saw the stubborn set of his jaw. This was the same proud man who'd defied death and was raging at being forced into accepting help from other people, even though he badly needed it. And she knew that James had been right on one score. There *was* something she'd failed to take into account when she'd come up with the original idea of a community centre; she'd consulted everyone but the real experts—the people for whom it was intended. How they felt hadn't entered the picture. From the perspective of Seth and his friends, it must seem not only a ludicrous omission but also the most unforgivable arrogance.

'We don't want outsiders interfering in our lives,' Seth continued, adding weight to her tardy conclusions.

'Is that all I am to you—an outsider?'

'No, girl, but only because I've come to know that there's more to you than meets the eye—which is more than I can say for them fancy colleagues of yours.' He sniffed. 'They don't care about how people like me live, Melody; they only care that we don't die on their doorsteps, because it would be bad for business.'

He was too close to the truth for comfort, but that didn't invalidate the benefits he might enjoy if the project went ahead. 'Surely by now you know that I care about you and how you live too much just to drop the idea,' she argued, buttoning up her coat. 'Can we talk about it more another day, and try to come up with a plan that's mutually acceptable?'

'Don't strike me as possible,' Seth muttered, tolerating a hug, 'but I reckon there's no harm in trying.'

'Leaving so soon?' James enquired, appearing from the kitchen with a wooden spatula in one hand and a dish towel tucked around his waist. 'Gee, what a shame! And here I was just about to invite you to stay for a plain, old-fashioned North American hamburger.'

Melody smiled sweetly. 'Another day, perhaps.'

He sighed with patent relief. 'Then let me show you out.'

'Don't bother. I hate to drag you away from the stove.'

'No bother,' he insisted, strong-arming her through the door and halfway down the path.

She had intended to make a discreet and graceful exit but his fingers, gouging her elbow through the down-filled fabric of her coat, changed her mind. 'I want you to know,' she snapped, extracting herself from his grip with energy, 'that if your poor father had an oven I'd probably stay long enough to shove you in it, head first.'

The creaky old gate almost snapped off its hinges from his kick. 'And I want you to know,' he ground out from between clenched teeth, 'that if you show up here again with your lady-of-the-manor-dispensing-alms-to-the-needy attitude I'll shove you and your delicacies——'

She planted her fists on her hips and stood toe to toe with him. 'Yes?'

'Aargh!' He swiped a hand over his face as though a fly were tormenting him, and gave a grunt of loathing. 'I disgust even me! Just go home, Melody, and please, if you come back again, do me a favour and make it some time when you know I won't be here. I don't much like the way I act when I'm around you.'

'I wish I could believe that,' she said wearily, 'but I don't. The fact is, you enjoy finding fault with everything I do.'

'That's not true!'

'Yes, it is. You conveniently overlook all the things about me that don't support your built-in conviction that I'm a rich, empty-headed socialite with a superficial set of values, and focus instead on things which might indicate a certain lack of judgement on my part but which don't in any way reflect a lack of respect for you or your father.'

'Such as what?' he demanded heatedly. 'Give me an example.'

'You insult me for the things I brought for Seth, simply because they're a bit more exotic than what he's used to, yet choose to ignore the time you invited yourself to dinner at my house and had to make do with food which was about as plain and unglamorous as you'll find anywhere. In fact, we've shared a number of meals together, not one of which has been exactly fancy, and you've never once heard me complain.'

'For God's sake, I'm talking about something more serious than food, Melody!' I'm talking about basic attitudes—about speaking different languages, coming from different worlds.'

'You're talking about dishonesty,' she said. 'In particular, your dishonesty. You'd rather lie to yourself than face up to the truth about me.'

He took a wary step back. 'What the hell is that supposed to mean?'

'That it's safer to label me as just another bored, rich, pitiful *bimbo* whom you find beneath contempt than it is for you to admit that I don't fit your stereotyped, preconceived, narrow-minded, unfair notions.'

'You forgot "unflattering",' he said, when she finally ran out of steam. 'And that's not all you forgot.'

It was her turn to back away. 'I don't know what you mean.'

'It's hardly likely I'd get sexually involved with the sort of woman you just described.'

'You don't get involved at all,' she replied sadly, cut to the heart by his description of the most special evening of her life. 'That's the whole problem, don't you see? You stand on the sidelines and make judgements instead of putting your theories to the test.'

He took a step closer, then another. His voice, when he spoke, was a raspy whisper. 'Oh, I put theory to the test all right, the night we made love, and if I'd been inclined to wonder about the results you certainly wasted no time setting me straight.' He pinned her with his gaze. 'I'm not the only one who doesn't get involved. Remember what you said, Melody? "Don't make something out of nothing, James. Tonight was no big deal." Or words to that effect.'

'I remember,' she said raggedly.

He covered the last few inches separating them and took her face in his hands. 'And you meant every word, of course.'

She nodded mutely and closed her eyes, appalled to find her anger dissolving into regret. It was pointless, and much too late, to admit differently. He'd made it clear enough that, although he found her desirable, he wasn't interested in marriage; and she knew now that she wasn't the kind who could settle for the few crumbs he might be coaxed into offering and make them last a lifetime. She was the all-or-nothing type.

She felt his breath fan her mouth and knew that if she so much as swayed towards him his lips would touch hers. To allow a kiss would be a mistake, she knew, yet, when the seconds ticked by and he made no effort to seize the opportunity, disappointment left her aching.

The night had been full of distant noises—the hoot of a ferry pulling away from the slip and heading across the Strait, the murmur of waves breaking below the sea wall, the muted blare of a radio from a passing car—but they were drowned out by the anguished throbbing of her heart.

She was on the brink of pulling herself free and breaking the agony of his spell, when he spoke. 'Look at me, Melody. Things aren't going any further until you do.'

Caught by surprise at his words, she obeyed him.

'That's better,' he said, and then he bridged the last tiny distance that separated them and finally kissed her, and it was worth any price she had to pay. His hands gentled to cup her face tenderly, the way a lover's should. His mouth cajoled and teased and seduced hers so completely that she didn't know where she found the strength to remain upright.

He unleashed such a desperate hunger in her that she wrapped her arms around his neck and clung to him and couldn't, for the life of her, contain the little moan of ecstasy that rose in her throat. All the bright and shiny stars that mere seconds before had been so securely anchored in the sky nosedived into Catherine wheels of oblivion. Her eyes fluttered closed again, too dazzled to bear the sight, and all of her—every bone, every muscle, every ounce of resistance—melted into one huge swirling tide of passion.

He didn't touch any other part of her. He didn't need to. His tongue and his lips made love to hers so thoroughly that they inflamed all of her, clouding her judgement and persuading her to view the hard edges of reality through rose-tinted lenses. Was it possible that he cared for her more than he was prepared to admit?

Intuition must have warned him of the direction her thoughts had taken because he withdrew his mouth, not abruptly, or reluctantly, but with slow and calculated cruelty, a little bit at a time.

She couldn't bear to lose that potent warmth, the sweet, wild taste of him. Another moan slipped free and she clung tighter, twining her fingers in his hair and clutching him for dear life. But she couldn't hold him. Unmoved, he slipped free and the cold winter air rushed in to supplant him, sweeping over her lips and down her throat to touch her heart with ice.

Even though there was no moon, enough light spilled from the cottage windows for her to see his face. Who would have thought such a severe, unsmiling mouth was capable of tenderness or passion? Obviously, whatever its effect on her, the kiss hadn't so much as sparked an ember in him.

'No big deal, right?' he mocked.

She dared not answer, afraid that her voice would break and betray her. To her consternation, her eyes filled and she felt her lip begin to tremble. Intent only on reaching her car and sparing them both the embarrassment of her making a complete fool of herself, she spun away from him—though not quickly enough, apparently, to hide the glimmer of her tears.

His hand shot out and jerked her to a halt. 'Tell me I'm right,' he insisted, and all at once his voice wasn't entirely steady. 'Tell me that you're too worldly to believe a superficial attraction like ours could ever develop into something deeper.'

One lone tear rolled down her face.

'Melody,' he muttered urgently, 'I don't see how you could possibly delude yourself into thinking we'd make a good match!'

'Of course you don't,' she cried. 'You're too blind to see the obvious, let alone scratch beneath the surface and figure out what goes on inside a person's head or heart.'

'Not blind,' he said, 'just realistic.'

'Realistic?' The quaver in her voice gave way to a travesty of laughter as anger stirred to life within her. 'Forget your theories about me—about us!—and take a good, hard look around you, James. Think about what you really see when you go back inside that miserable little cottage...'

'It might strike you as miserable, but it's the place Seth calls home.'

'And while you're at it,' she went on, strengthened by the gathering force of her anger, 'take a look at the man you call Father, and think about the sort of life he leads. Oh, but I forgot, you don't call him Father, do you? That's too personal, too close for comfort. No matter, it's just a name, and nothing you call him will do a blessed thing to make his life less empty than it already is. Think about how he spent Christmas, James. Ask yourself why he was hanging around in the rain, half drunk and itching for a fight, the night he got run down by a car.'

'I wasn't to blame for that,' James snarled.

'Good. Then run back to the Caribbean with a clear conscience, or, better yet, Timbuktu. It's further away, and a lot safer. Seth won't show up unexpectedly, and you can be damn sure I won't, so you won't have to cope with the unwelcome burden of our needs or affections.'

'My father doesn't want my affection.'

'Your father would give his right arm to be close to you, but don't let that slow you down. He's managed this long without having a son he could count on. What's another empty thirty years?'

A muscle twitched in the granite set of his jaw. 'Are you done?'

She looked at him, and wondered if it would take thirty years before she could forget how easy it would have been to spend a lifetime loving him. Anger seeped into despair. 'Oh, yes,' she said numbly. 'I'm done. Goodbye, James.'

He watched until the winking red tail-lights of her car disappeared around the curve of the old sea wall and, all the time, he told himself that his primary feeling was one of relief. From the outset she had been an irritant and, even if it had taken somewhat desperate measures to achieve, at least he was rid of her. He didn't for a moment doubt that. There had been a world of finality in the way she had said goodbye, then slid behind the wheel of her car and driven off without once looking back.

If he hadn't been so bloody annoyed, he'd have smiled at the thought of what had just transpired. The setting: a back-street on the shabby side of town, with a seventy-thousand-dollar sports coupé parked outside a weather-beaten old shack that wasn't worth a tenth that amount even by today's inflated prices. The characters: her, snuggled inside her iridescent green and gold down-filled coat, feet warm in fleece-lined boots imported from Italy, and skin perfumed with the best Paris had to offer. And him with a tea-towel draped around his waist to protect the jeans he'd picked off the shelves of the local discount outlet when he'd realised sorting out his father's affairs was going to involve more than paying duty visits at the hospital and chasing up insurance claims.

It had been a ludicrous scene all round, but then, why not? From the outset, his whole association with Melody Worth had been preposterous, and it was absurd for him to be standing there in the freezing cold, wondering if there might be a grain of truth in anything she'd said.

Impatient with the whole damn world, he strode back to the house, wincing as the hinges moaned, first on the gate, then again, more stridently, on the front door.

'You feel one tenth as bad as you look,' Seth observed from under lowered brows, 'then I feel sorry for you.'

If that wasn't the last straw—Seth's pity on top of her contempt! 'I'm hungry,' James snapped. 'Let's eat.'

The hamburgers tasted like sawdust, the beer as flat as water, yet Seth seemed to relish every mouthful. James cleared his throat. 'What—er—what did you have for dinner on Christmas Day, Seth?'

'Don't rightly remember,' Seth replied, demolishing the last morsel on his plate. 'Nothing special.'

The hamburger sat like lead in the pit of James's stomach. 'How would you like it,' he asked, 'if I took you out for a decent meal while I'm here?'

'Hell, boy, I don't need that,' Seth protested. 'It's treat enough for me having someone else do the cooking. Never thought I'd say this, but there's times when I miss your mother. There's something about a woman's touch...' He frowned, and pushed his chair away from the table and swung it to face the fire. 'I don't know, it sort of rounds a man's life off properly. She makes a place feel like home—fills it with the smell of good cooking that makes a meal worth waiting for.'

James didn't want to hear this. 'You don't need a woman for things like that, Seth. There's no mystery to following a recipe.'

'Maybe not, but a woman's got a mystery to her that nothing else can quite replace.' He grinned, a little wistfully, it seemed to James. 'I sometimes think that, if your mother hadn't upped and run off never to be heard from again the day after you left school, I might have found myself knocking on her door again some day.'

'Not just because you missed her cooking, I hope! As I understand it, the pair of you never did anything but fight.'

'Ah, yes, well...' Seth reached out and massaged his leg thoughtfully. 'She was too young to know how best to handle me, and I was too daft to understand that, and sometimes fighting's just another way of loving a person. I reckon if the chance came my way again I'd do things somewhat different the second time around. If truth be known, I didn't have the first idea how to show a woman I loved her back then.' He stared into the fire a while, then turned to James. 'Reckon you got the same problem.'

'I don't have any problems,' James said.

Seth cackled. 'If you think that, then you're worse than daft—you're bloody stupid. We all got problems, son, and what it really comes down to in the end is learning which ones we can do something about—and then finding the guts to deal with them.'

James switched his gaze to the flames dancing up the chimney, not because he was the kind who deluded himself into believing he'd discover anything as obscure as the meaning of life leaping in their depths, but because it was preferable to returning his father's rather penetrating stare, that was all.

He'd have fastened his attention on the room at large except that, each time he tried, Melody's words accused him all over again, and found him guilty. She was right. The place was a dump. He didn't know how his father stood it.

As for the conversation he'd just had with his father, not only was it the longest he could recall their ever having shared, it was also the most disturbing.

He flung himself to his feet, feeling, suddenly, as if the walls were closing in on him. 'I need some exercise and a breath of air. Will you be OK by yourself for a while?'

Seth blinked, as though he'd forgotten James was there to begin with. 'Hell, yes, boy! I'm used to being by myself.'

It wasn't just the walls closing in, James thought resentfully, striding down the road to the sea wall. His whole damned life was coming apart at the seams, its efficient, uncluttered design disintegrating into a mass of complications that multiplied with each additional day he spent here.

And he knew who was to blame. He must remember to thank her, in the unlikely event that he ever saw her again.

CHAPTER EIGHT

MELODY didn't expect to see James again. Even less did she expect him to show up at her shop the following week in the company of city alderman Charles Raines, one of her grandfather's old golfing buddies. From the way James stood at near-attention and stared over her head, she could only suppose he'd been dragged in against his better judgement. Intrigued despite herself, she did her best to ignore him and directed an enquiring glance at Charles.

'No,' the alderman smiled, shaking his head at her unspoken question, 'I'm not here to rent anything today, Melody. I've come to talk business of another kind. You've been making headlines, young lady, with this proposal of yours to promote a neighbourhood community centre, and it's been brought to the attention of the city fathers. Most of Monday's council meeting was devoted to discussing its merits.'

Flipping up the brim of a flower-decked straw hat and hanging it on one of the black velvet display pads of her antique hat rack, Melody flung James a brief, antagonistic glare. 'In view of the company you're keeping these days, I can only suppose you're against it too, Charles.'

'Not at all.' Charles climbed on to a high stool next to the counter and hooked his feet around its rungs. 'In fact, you've got almost everyone on council behind you.'

'I hear a "but",' she said despondently. Life was full of 'buts', these days, especially if James was in the picture.

'Well, not exactly, but it's a municipal election year and most of us will be out looking for votes, so naturally we're not about to support a project that's going to upset people.'

She dusted off a cream silk cloche and hung it next to the straw hat. 'So what's the problem, Charles?'

'Council is willing to offer a ninety-nine-year lease on the property for a nominal sum, if you can raise enough funds to ensure completion of the remodelling.'

'That has always been our intention.'

'There's more,' Charles said, and cleared his throat nervously, although James's expression remained carefully neutral.

Melody's suspicions ballooned into certainty. Something unpleasant was in the offing. 'I knew there would be,' she said.

'The thing is, municipal elections are coming up, and we have to be able to convince the voters that we aren't supporting extravagant schemes that have no merit beyond spending taxpayers' money. You know, of course, that the site in question has been designated a heritage building, and that there are rigid guidelines regarding its use.'

'Red tape,' Melody declared, a good deal more airily than she felt. 'We expected it.'

James chose that moment to put in his two cents' worth. 'No doubt she also expects to cut her way through it by greasing the right palms,' he observed, treating her much as he had the day of the TV interview—as if she didn't quite exist.

Well, two could play at that game! 'Why is he here?' she asked Charles.

'Because, in order for the project to get the green light, you'll have to agree to work with a panel of experts comprised of an architect, someone from the city planner's department, a structural engineer and, of course, a representative from the heritage society.'

'He's a naval architect. What does he know about buildings?'

For an experienced politician, Charles looked disturbingly flustered. 'Council insists that, because of the publicity surrounding his accident, Seth Logan be invited to sit on the committee as spokesman for the beneficiaries. And also...' He cleared his throat again. 'Well, my dear...'

Melody sighed. 'Here comes the "but", Charles, right?'

He tugged at the knot in his tie as though it were half strangling him. 'Perhaps. I'm afraid too many people saw that television interview, my dear. Unfortunately, it left some with the impression that the real purpose of providing a facility that's badly needed has been lost sight of in the tug of war between two people whose personal relationship has gone sour. In order to justify its support, council has to be able to demonstrate that joint co-operation from both—er—parties...has risen above petty differences. We want to see you and James working together on this for the common good.'

'And I've agreed,' James said.

'Whatever for?' Melody knew the tone of her voice underscored the dismay on her face.

'Because my roots are here and I've got a personal stake in the outcome,' James informed her smugly. 'I'm also smart, educated, articulate and not afraid to speak my mind.'

'Not to mention sickeningly modest,' Melody snapped.

'Try to get along, children,' Charles begged, dabbing his forehead with a linen handkerchief. 'Your co-operation is vital to the successful outcome of this entire scheme.'

At that moment, Melody wanted nothing so much as to indulge in an outright battle with James. It would have afforded her the utmost satisfaction to have scratched his eyes out, in fact, and she had to remind herself that she'd been brought up by a different set of rules. 'I'm willing to do whatever has to be done, Charles,' she said. 'You didn't have to bring him along to add weight to your presentation.'

'I wanted to make sure you both understand what's expected of you,' Charles said with evident relief. 'There's no room for personal grievances here. Whatever your private feelings towards one another, they have to be left behind during committee proceedings. Can you agree to that?'

'Yes,' James said.

No! Melody wanted to cry. She couldn't sit across a table from James and present rational arguments, no matter how worthy the cause, because her response to him had never, not from the first, been rational. She responded to him on an entirely different level, one governed by emotions and instincts not easily tamed by logic.

And yet... She sighed in defeat. If she didn't agree at least to try to go along with Charles's demands, wasn't she falling into the very trap that could well put an end to the success of a project that had already cost her dearly?

'I agree that your father should be involved, but I'd much prefer that you didn't have to be drawn into things,' she felt compelled to admit.

James didn't try to hide his grin. 'That's because you think you can sweet talk your way around my father more easily than you can around me.'

'No, it's because you hold us in the utmost contempt,' she replied. 'You divorced yourself from this town, and everyone in it, years ago. However,' she amended hastily, seeing the way Charles's lips tightened in disapproval, 'if you can tolerate having to work with me, I can certainly put up with you for the short time you're likely to stick around.'

Charles's mouth relaxed into a smile. 'Your grandfather would be proud of you, my dear. You're a woman after his own heart.' He reached over the counter to pat her hand. 'The first meeting has been scheduled for next Tuesday evening. See you both then, seven o'clock sharp at City Hall.'

It came all too soon.

Melody had expected the atmosphere at the meeting to be a little awkward. It was, after all, only the second time she and James had seen each other since her rather dramatic departure from his father's cottage. But she had thought herself well prepared. She arrived just as the meeting was about to begin, thereby sparing herself the necessity of having to indulge in social chit-chat with anyone. She smiled at Seth, and spared James a civil nod because she wasn't about to fuel the gossip mills with rumours that she was harbouring a grudge, but she drew the line at sitting with him and his father. Ignoring Seth's gesture of disappointment, she chose a seat at the opposite end of the table.

Thank the lord! Melody thought fervently, when the meeting swung into high gear immediately. Those awkward first moments were behind them. The rest of the evening would be devoted to business and once the meeting was over she planned to be out of the building before anyone had time to notice she was gone.

How did it happen, then, that her finely tuned strategy failed abysmally within seconds of the meeting's close, and she found herself coerced into sharing a late dinner with Seth and James? Not that James rushed to extend the invitation. He merely stood there like the proverbial block of stone, a frozen expression on his handsome face, as Seth thrust his wheelchair directly into her flight path and stopped her dead in her tracks before she'd covered the first five yards to the door.

'Hold up there, girl! Where's the fire?' he wanted to know.

'I'm starving, Seth,' she explained. 'I didn't have time for dinner before I came here tonight.'

'Good! Then you can have a meal with us. James is taking me to one of them fancy places that people like you and him eat at all the time.'

She'd *rather* starve! 'That's wonderful, Seth, and I wouldn't dream of intruding on such a special occasion.'

'Reckon it would be a sight more special if a pretty woman like you was there, too,' he wheedled. 'Reckon it'd make folks sit up and take notice to see me being wheeled into the joint by my favourite lady in the whole world. Or is it,' he wondered slyly, 'that you're ashamed to be seen in public with me?'

'Of course I'm not ashamed!'

'Then it's settled. James, what are you standing there for like a man with his tongue stuck to his tonsils? She can come with us, can't she?'

James wore a dark business suit, immaculately tailored and sleekly styled. His shirt was snowy cotton, his tie discreetly patterned burgundy on pewter silk. His skin glowed; his hair gleamed. He looked as handsome as a movie star and as regally distant as the head of state of some very unfriendly foreign country.

'By all means,' he allowed coolly, and inclined his head towards the door. 'Shall we go?'

'I'll take my own car,' Melody said.

He suffered to glance at her. 'Don't be absurd. There's no point in taking two cars when one will do the job. You can pick yours up later.' And without giving her time to argue, let alone agree, he swept Seth and his wheelchair out into the frosty night. Left with no alternative short of sprinting for her own car like a frightened rabbit, Melody followed.

'Sit in the front, Melody,' James ordered as they approached the rented sedan.

'Oh, no! I'd rather not.'

'You don't have a lot of choice,' Seth said. 'I can stretch out this damned cast a lot easier in the back than I can in them itty-bitty seats in the front.' He chuckled. 'When I was young and up to no good, they knew how to build cars so a fellow could have his girl practically sitting on his lap as he drove, but all these new-fangled contraptions are good for is getting a man from here to there as uncomfortably as possible.'

'Oh, I don't know,' James remarked silkily, sliding an oblique glance Melody's way. 'I dare say if these compact cars could talk they'd surprise us all with what they've witnessed. If you ask me, they're designed to keep a man safe from unwarranted attack. But get in anyway, Melody. You're too much a lady to take advantage of me while I'm at the wheel, I'm sure.'

She hated him, she really did!

The Crab Island Inn was arguably the best seafood restaurant in the area, and certainly the most picturesque. Situated at the end of a narrow spit, it boasted magnificent water views from the bay windows lining six of the walls in its octagonal dining-room. A floor-to-ceiling fireplace occupied the eighth wall, while a glass-enclosed solarium on the opposite wall housed an aquarium and a profusion of flowering plants that brought a splash of colour to the drabness of winter. A dance-floor about the size of a bed-sheet occupied the middle of the room, with music supplied by a pianist.

James did not seem disposed to appreciate the setting, or to linger over social niceties. In fact a speedy end to the evening appeared to be uppermost in his mind. 'Cocktail?' he practically growled, barely allowing Melody time to settle in her chair.

She shook her head. 'No, thank you.'

'Wine, then?'

'No.'

He scanned the wine list anyway. 'Bring us a bottle of the white Bordeaux,' he told the waiter.

The wine arrived, was displayed and uncorked with great ceremony, and a splash finally poured for James's approval. Seth, Melody noticed, watched the entire procedure with fascinated disbelief.

James went through the ritual of sniffing and tasting. 'That's fine,' he decided.

'It's just as well you think so,' Seth observed, 'seeing as how you just took a hefty swig of the stuff.'

Eyeing Seth as if he were a new and unusual form of life, the waiter cleared his throat. 'Er—do you wish to order now, sir?'

'Yes,' James said.

'Melody,' Seth muttered urgently, 'this menu's all written in a foreign language. How's a man supposed to know what he's putting in his stomach?'

'Read the small print,' she whispered back. 'That's the English translation.'

'It don't make much sense, either! About the only words I recognise is "clams" and "halibut".' He looked up at the waiter and cackled with malicious delight at the man's frozen expression. 'Reckon that makes it easy! I'll have either clams or halibut.'

Clearly accustomed to a more discriminating clientele, the waiter curled his lip and touched the tip of his pen to Seth's menu. 'There is a choice of smoked or fresh clams, sir, unless, of course, you were referring to the chowder, which is a speciality of the house. And the halibut is either pan-fried in herbed lemon butter and sprinkled with capers, or baked in a brandied cream sauce with leeks and served with nasturtium flowers.'

'God give me strength!' Seth exclaimed. 'You're talking to an old fisherman here, sonny, not some half-wit that can't tell the difference, so don't try palming me off with something you've had to dress up in fancy clothes. I want halibut, plain and simple—with potatoes, not flowers!'

Throughout the exchange, James leaned back in his chair, not a flicker of expression on his face, and watched Melody, who was having a hard time containing her amusement.

'Madam?' The waiter hovered hopefully at her elbow, pen poised.

'I'll have the halibut, too,' she said. 'Exactly as my friend ordered—plain and simple.'

'Make mine the same,' James said, 'with the addition of a Caesar salad. In fact...' he glanced across the table at Melody, and it seemed to her that the ghost of a smile had warmed his eyes, too '...why don't we make it salad for three?'

'That would be nice,' she said politely.

'How long before we eat?' Seth wanted to know.

'The main course will take about twenty minutes, sir,' the long-suffering waiter advised, preparing to escape. 'As I'm sure you appreciate, good food takes time to prepare. Your salad, however, will be served shortly.'

'Well, until it is, I'm off to check out that aquarium,' Seth decided. 'You two can keep each other entertained till I get back, I'm sure.'

Melody wished she shared his confidence. The silence hummed between her and James, taut as a wire under stress. She glanced up and caught him watching her. He immediately transferred his attention to the tireless roll of the surf on the sand, leaving her to study his profile at her leisure.

Would some other man's image one day be super-imposed over her memories of James, his body hard and powerful in the firelight, her own supple and compliant beneath his hot, compelling mouth? She thought not, and endured a spasm of anguish at the knowledge.

He sipped his wine and continued to gaze moodily out at the floodlit stretch of beach beyond the window. 'We're not doing a very good job of entertaining each other, are we?' he muttered.

Did he think, all things considered, that they should be? Or was he hoping she'd grovel for a kind word to ease her suffering? 'I'm afraid not.'

'Are you embarrassed by my father's behaviour?'

'No, James,' she replied, insulted. 'I like your father very much and I find his attitudes refreshing. Why do you ask? Because *you're* embarrassed?'

'Not at all, but then I don't come from——'

'My side of the tracks,' she finished tiredly. 'I know, James. You make sure I never forget it.'

'Would you like to dance?'

It was the most indifferently uttered invitation she'd ever received. 'No,' she assured him. 'Your father is your guest tonight and I'm just someone you got stuck with, so, his directions notwithstanding, please *don't* feel you have to entertain me.'

James smiled with gentle irony, and swirled the wine in his glass. 'I seldom feel I have to do anything, Melody, any more than I make a habit of coercing other people into something they don't want to do. Can you say the same? Or are you hoping that your friends on council will sweep my objections under the carpet and allow you to barge full-steam ahead with the plans to force-feed your charitable and no doubt worthy intentions down the throats of my father and his friends?'

'I knew it was a mistake to agree to this dinner,' Melody said, setting down her glass untouched and standing up.

'Dear me!' he said with mock-regret. 'Leaving so soon, my lady?'

She tugged her slim-fitting skirt more snugly around her hips and injected a note of scorn into her voice. 'No. I've merely decided that dancing's preferable to having to hold a conversation with you, that's all—assuming the offer still holds.'

'As you wish.' He scraped back his chair, his smile about as conciliatory as petrol poured on an already flaming fire. 'Should I take out life insurance first?'

'Absolutely not,' she snapped, dragging him on to the floor with rather more aggression than was, perhaps, strictly ladylike. 'I plan to murder you some other time, when no one's around to witness the happy event.'

'If you find me so impossible,' he murmured, slipping his arm around her waist and settling his hand in the small of her back, 'why did you agree to work with me on the committee?'

He danced superbly. Why was she surprised? He did *everything* superbly, right down to making love to a woman and then dropping her. 'Because I had no choice. And I don't wish to discuss the matter further.'

'And why,' he persisted, undaunted, 'if you're as fond of my father as you'd like everyone to believe, do you insist on going ahead with this damned community shelter nonsense? Neither he nor his friends are any more keen on it than I am.'

'I happen to disagree. I can't speak for his friends, of course, but I think that Seth will throw his support behind it once he understands its broader concepts.'

James snorted with amusement and twirled her merrily around the perimeter of the dance-floor. 'Whatever makes you believe that, my dear lady?'

How was it that such a sexy drawl of a voice could convey such scornful ridicule? 'He's open to new ideas and willing to listen to someone else's point of view,' she retorted, a mite breathlessly. 'You, on the other hand, are incapable of objective reasoning and far too biased to see anything beyond the limits of your narrow-minded prejudice. Furthermore——'

'Melody,' he corrected her softly, gathering her close as the pianist swung to a slower, dreamier number, 'I see further down the road than you can possibly imagine. I see my well-ordered life shot to hell all because I came here to take care of a man I barely know.'

He folded her hand against his chest, right next to the strong, steady beat of his heart. His voice ruffled the crown of her head, his other arm tightened around her waist, and that old potent attraction she worked so hard to suppress sprang to new life, all the more insistent, it seemed, because it was so obviously doomed.

'And I find myself,' he continued, 'getting embroiled in other people's lives, and forming attachments I had not expected and most assuredly do not want.'

There was no question that she and James were adversaries, pure and simple. The only problem was that their bodies seemed not to know it and were bent on a different course. Perfectly attuned and anticipating exactly what their next move would be, they ignored the words being bandied about, and nested together in unbridled delight, flowing effortlessly together over the dance-floor.

The fingers once situated in the small of her back rode up to press along her ribs, bringing her breasts into full contact with the hard texture of his chest. Could he tell, Melody wondered dazedly, that her nipples were stirring to awareness? Did he know that the gentle nudge of his knee against her thigh sent a flood of heat quivering down and provoked a helpless spasm of longing to clench inside her, or that a delicate prickle of sensation danced across the palm of her hand where it curved around his neck?

'If you're trying to sweet talk me into dropping the project, James,' she almost stammered, 'I'm afraid you've sadly underestimated my determination.'

'I'm afraid I've sadly underestimated you all round. Whatever your faults—and there are a few, I've noticed!—you're a quality product, Melody.'

Futilely, she tried to stoke the embers of resentment. 'Oh, please, not that old theme again!'

'I'm not talking about money or upbringing this time. I'm talking about decent human kindness. Quite frankly, a lot of the women I know would have run for the hills at Seth's performance with that waiter.'

And how many women do you know? she itched to ask. 'He was being himself,' she said instead, 'and that's something I understand. No one should have to apologise for that, James, no matter how much money he does or doesn't have.'

He tilted away from her far enough to look down into her eyes as though hoping that, if he searched diligently enough, he'd find lies instead of truth. Screwing up her courage, she gazed back.

'Our salads are waiting and so is Seth,' he said, restoring distance between them with an abruptness that briefly left her staggering. 'And dancing wasn't such a bright idea after all. Good God, another minute of all this smoochy music and proximity, and I'd be making admissions I'd regret tomorrow.'

She was in cahoots with the devil! She was a devious angel saying all the right things and knowing exactly the right buttons to press. And those eyes, all soulful, sympathetic honesty... Oh, brother! He ought to know better than to sink into their treacherous depths.

'Let's eat and get this over with,' he said, quelling the stab of guilt that arose inside at Seth's quickly covered disappointment. He'd make it up to the old man before he left town. They'd go for one last, glorious blow-out together, without the distraction of Melody's company to spoil things.

But over the course of the next three weeks, it took all his considerable will-power to stay away from her. During the days, it wasn't so bad. He was able to keep busy making the house more comfortable. Those infernal committee meetings, however, were another matter entirely. How he got through them, he didn't know. How he was going to see them through to conclusion was an even bigger mystery, especially since they threatened to go on indefinitely with nothing being accomplished.

'Can we please quit floundering around and get this show on the road?' he enquired of the assembly at large, as the fourth meeting threatened to bog down in political debate. 'Any fool knows social conscience and balanced budgets make poor bedfellows, and I'm getting tired of listening to you all bewailing the fact.'

'You could always resign,' Melody suggested, with an innocent little smile that riled him worse than ever.

'Believe me, I'd gladly leave you to hang yourself in red tape if it would get me out of here faster,' he informed her.

'Wishful thinking isn't going to help matters, James,' she purred, 'but if it's all turning out to be more than you can handle, consider yourself excused.'

A discreet 'ahem' from someone further down the table reminded him that he had an audience. Wrestling his features along pleasanter lines, he returned her smile. 'No, thanks. I have an ingrained resistance to walking out on something when it's only half finished. It smacks too much of running away. Perhaps if we were to bend our energies to finding solutions, instead of focusing on problems . . . ?'

He'd finally pressed the right button. At the very next meeting, Melody presented the committee with the perfect way to overcome obstacles that he had long since concluded were going to keep him chained there indefinitely.

It happened halfway through March after a day of mild spring sunshine that had daffodils and forsythia bursting all over town. Earlier that same afternoon, James had realised with a sense of shock that it had been more than two months since he'd come back to Port Armstrong. No wonder there were times when he almost felt at home in the place!

'There are those among us,' Melody announced, staring at him from her position at the other end of the table and daring him with her big, beautiful eyes to find fault with *this* suggestion, 'who object strenuously to the indignity of forcing so-called charity on people who have not expressly asked for help. And there are others who feel, as I do, that waiting until people reach that point of desperation is equally insensitive and demeaning. On top of that, both sides are concerned at the potential expense a project of this nature entails. Well, I believe I've come up with a way to resolve everyone's misgivings.'

Very smooth and businesslike, Melody, James thought. Very professional indeed!

No one would guess from listening to her cool, articulate reasoning that she was capable of more fire and passion than any other three women put together. Nor would they guess that underneath that trim little black suit and plain silk blouse she had a body as delicate and fragrant as gardenias, or that her breasts were small and perfect, her thighs as smooth as cream.

Perspiration dotted his forehead at the memory. He swore inaudibly and stabbed his pencil on the notepad in front of him, right through the heart carved on the bow of the sailing-boat he'd drawn. Damn, oh, damn! Why hadn't some other man married her before now, and taken her out of temptation's way?

And what would these worthy representatives of Port Armstrong society think if they knew that one of their number was finding himself embarrassingly aroused by the lady currently enthralling them with the brilliance of her intellect?

No doubt he'd be tarred, feathered, and run out of town on a rail!

'Absolutely!' the man seated next to him suddenly crowed, leaving James to wonder briefly if he'd been insane enough to voice his thoughts aloud. 'It's the only answer.'

'Ideal,' a woman with loose-fitting dentures brayed. 'Only a fool could object to it.'

Seth, ever Melody's greatest ally except in the matter of her pet project, was thumping approval on the table.

'Reckon even I can go along with that, girl. I know a couple of men who could run the kitchen. One of them cooked for years on the tug-boats until arthritis made him more of a hindrance on board than a help. And there's plenty of us know how to wield a hammer and saw. We've worked with wood most of our lives in one way or another. 'Course, we're not much good shimmying up ladders any more, but we could take care of a lot of the finishing ourselves.'

'I hoped you'd feel like that,' Melody said, bestowing such a sweet smile on his father that James felt envy, raw and acrid, rise in his throat. 'I even wondered if, once the building's finished, some of you might be interested in setting up a workshop where members of the public could bring small antiques and such for repair and restoration. It would be a source of revenue that could go towards the upkeep of the facility.'

'A free meal once in a while would sit a lot more easily in my stomach if I knew I'd done something towards earning it,' Seth admitted, 'and I know the rest of the boys feel the same. It ain't so much that we don't want a place where we can go when we find ourselves at loose ends; it's the idea that we're being treated like kids who need baby-sitting that's put us off. But this way...' He grinned and shook his head. 'Hell, I'm not too proud to trade one good deal for another.'

Melody smiled at him again. 'Naturally, we'll continue the fund-raising, so the cost of initial supplies and labour will be covered.'

'How'd you feel about us setting up down the street, Melody, girl?'

'I can't think of neighbours I'd like better, Seth.'

And she followed that with another dazzling smile that remained impervious to the scowl James sent her way.

'One last thing before we wrap this up,' Charles Raines announced, producing a batch of envelopes from his briefcase. 'The mayor is hosting the annual Port Armstrong spring ball a week from Saturday. As a gesture of thanks for the time and effort that you've devoted to these meetings, you're all invited to attend. Considering the enormous progress we've made tonight, it strikes me as a timely occasion on which to celebrate.' He leaned forward to address Seth. 'The mayor, Mr Logan, particularly expressed the hope that you will be able to attend.'

How very astute of the mayor, James thought uncharitably. That should garner him a few more votes come election day.

'Me?' Pride held brief reign before reality set in and dimmed the eagerness in Seth's eyes. Uncertainly, he appealed to James, a quaver in his voice. 'I don't know as how I'd rightly fit in by myself.'

The door to freedom clanged shut. 'We'll both be there.' James bared his teeth in a feeble grin, and privately recited a litany of curses that would have made a stevedore blush.

God help him, he felt protective towards the old man. Affectionate, even! What next? And where was it all going to end, for crying out loud?

CHAPTER NINE

JAMES had attended more than a few upper-crust social gatherings since his rise to professional prominence, but never had he seen quite as ostentatious a display of wealth as that at Port Armstrong's spring ball. 'A jewel thief could retire on the pickings to be heisted from this crowd,' he muttered to Seth as they entered the foyer of the Ambassador Hotel's grand ballrooms.

'Look at them dresses!' Seth breathed, eyeing a swirl of beads and sequins that floated past. 'A man could practically shave in the reflection!'

James grinned. 'Speaking of sartorial splendour, you look pretty nifty yourself, old man!'

'It's the walking-stick,' Seth said, brandishing his silver-headed cane pridefully. 'It gives a man——'

'A weapon. Quit waving it around like that, Seth, before you brain somebody. What do you want to drink?'

'Champagne,' Seth said.

'*Champagne*?'

'When a man's all dressed up in a monkey suit, it don't look right for him to be swigging a beer.'

'I guess not.' James's laugh had heads turning their way. 'Let's find you a seat somewhere out of the traffic flow, then I'll join the line-up at the bar.'

'Find Melody first,' Seth said. 'I've waited nearly seventy years to taste champagne. Reckon I can wait another few minutes.'

'It'll take a lot longer than that to track her down. This crowd fills two ballrooms, Seth. We might miss her altogether.'

'Then why didn't you phone and ask her to come with us in the first place, instead of being so dad-blamed stubborn? I want to sit with her and I want to see what she's wearing.' Seth waved the cane around again, scattering those standing nearest. 'She'll put this lot in the shade.'

Afraid Seth might be right, James hoped he'd manage to avoid her. He wanted this evening to be a very special one, one his father could relish and regale his cronies with for the next ten years, so by all means let there be champagne and music, diamonds and designer dresses, well-known faces and headline names. But please, lord, let it stop short of Melody imprinting disturbing, unforgettable images in the corners of his mind. There was a limit to how much punishment he could take and he was suffering enough already at the thought of what the aftermath of tonight might mean to his father tomorrow.

It was ironical that, at this late date, incipient family ties threatened to bind the two men. Their goals had never been more disparate, their disagreements never more heated, yet James had experienced pangs of guilt as he'd made plans to get on with his own life. Deep down, he knew regret and a certain sadness for lost time where his father was concerned. Allowing himself to dwell on what might have been with Melody, had things been different, burdened him with too much emotional overload and threatened the splendid isolation that formed the parameters of his life.

The Ambassador Hotel had been built in the grand old days when labour and materials were cheap. The ballrooms and adjacent foyer and reception room were hung with silk wall panels and imported crystal chandeliers. The furnishings were period antiques, and the hardwood floors glowed like fine brandy. It was the perfect setting for an evening of glamour and romance.

So why, Melody wondered, touching up her lipstick in the ladies' powder-room, did she feel dejected and dowdy? Her dress had seemed downright fabulous hanging on the mannequin in the shop where she'd bought it. Softly draped ivory satin touched with a blush of pink, it cinched her waist then blossomed into a shower of petals to her ankles, and had her name written all over it—or so she'd thought. Pastels always suited her dark hair and fair complexion, so what had gone wrong this time?

Whatever it was, it affected her perceptions of her escort, too. A man she'd dated casually off and on for more than a year, Robert was the kind a normal woman would snap up without a second glance—nice, cultured, gallant; nice, socially aware, politically correct; nice . . .

Dear Robert; his parents had done such a good job raising him! Why couldn't she be more appreciative of that, instead of comparing him invidiously to James Logan?

Perhaps, if James had been in evidence, she might find reason to feel differently. Perhaps, set beside a man of Robert's sterling qualities, James's flaws might appear less forgivable and he might not seem so incomparably desirable and right for her. And perhaps the fact that she hadn't so much as caught a glimpse of his face to-night was the reason she felt so let down.

She fluffed her fringe and plastered a smile on her face. It promised to be a long and arduous evening, but she owed it to Robert not to let her feelings show. There were probably at least a dozen other women who'd have been only too pleased to take her place at his side, given the chance, and he was too nice to be left wondering what he'd done to deserve someone who clearly wished she were somewhere else, with someone else.

'Sorry to keep you waiting,' she said, joining the patient Robert in the foyer.

His warm brown eyes crinkled at the edges when he smiled, something he did often. 'Don't be,' he said, tucking her hand protectively into the crook of his elbow. 'You're worth waiting for. By the way, the Frasers are here and are saving us seats at their table.'

'How nice,' Melody replied, and winced. There it was again, that word 'nice'. It popped up all the time whenever James wasn't around. No doubt, if she thought about it realistically, she'd have a far *nicer* life without him than she could ever hope to find with him.

'Quite a few new faces this year,' Robert observed, weaving his elegant six-foot-one frame through the crush of guests and making sure none of them stepped on the toes of her pink satin pumps.

'Oh?' She craned her neck, hoping to catch a glimpse of one face in particular, but not even her three-inch heels gave her the height advantage she needed.

After dinner, the mayor gave his annual address, and shortly after that the dancing began. It was probably about an hour later, just as she and Robert were passing the bar on their way to catch a breath of cooler air in the foyer, that a figure hobbled forward and interspersed itself between Melody and her partner.

'I knew,' a familiar voice crowed, 'that we'd find you sooner or later. Why have you been avoiding us, Melody, girl?'

'I haven't,' she insisted, but the fact of the matter was that she might well have passed him by and ignored him without meaning to do so. In full dinner suit, with his thick grey hair neatly trimmed and his jaw so scrupulously clean-shaven that it shone, this was not the Seth

Logan she knew. 'My goodness, Seth, I hardly recognise you!'

'Pretty spiffy, eh?' He cackled and swung his cane with cavalier abandon. 'Reckon you never thought to see me dressed up to the nines like this, did you?'

'No, I didn't,' she admitted, 'but, now that I have, let me tell you you should do it more often. Seth, you look . . .' She flung up her hands and laughed. 'You look fabulously distinguished and handsome!'

'And you're a picture.' Switching his cane to his other hand, Seth raised her fingertips and kissed them with such courtly grace that Melody felt embarrassingly close to tears. For all that they'd shared together over the last two months, he had never before initiated physical contact of any kind. At best, he had tolerated a hug or a very occasional peck on the cheek.

'Thank you, Seth.' She swallowed the lump in her throat and blinked. At her side, Robert gave a polite little 'ahem', a gentle reminder that she was forgetting her manners. 'Robert, this is my friend, Seth Logan. We met when he was hospitalised last January.'

'I remember,' Robert replied, shaking hands with impeccable civility. 'How are you feeling now, sir?'

'Back on my pins and about as good as new,' Seth said. 'Melody, why haven't you been to see me lately?'

'I've been busy,' she lied. 'I don't know where the time has gone these last few weeks. All of a sudden, it's spring, yet it seems that the last time I looked at the calendar it was still January. But we have spoken on the phone, Seth.'

'T'ain't the same.'

'No, it isn't, which is one reason I'm very glad to see you now. I was hoping you'd decide to come tonight. Did James—er—is he here, too?'

'He's here,' Seth said. 'In fact, he's been propping up the bar behind you for the last five minutes, pretending he ain't listening in.' Seth gave a flourish with his cane and cocked an eye at Robert. 'Reckon you and I could have a beer together, my lad, and let these two take a spin around the floor?'

'Watch the damned cane, Seth!' James growled, stepping forward into view. 'And stop trying to organise my life. I'm capable of fulfilling my social obligations without any prompting from you.'

'Good. You'll know where to find us when you're done, then.' Seth grinned and lowered his voice. 'He's a bit peeved, if you want the truth,' he confided to Melody. 'I sent him looking for you when we first got here, and he got trapped by that man-eater that sells fur coats in your shopping arcade.'

'Ariadne?' Melody knew the other tenants had received invitations to the ball in recognition of their fund-raising efforts, but the only one she'd seen so far was Roger.

'That's the one. Hanging half out of her dress she was, and climbing all over him. Thought I was going to have to come to his rescue. 'Course, it could've been a lot worse; could've been the other one that got her hooks into him—the one that looks as if she swallowed a sour pickle.'

'I should have rented you a muzzle as well as a walking-stick,' James lamented. 'Shut up, Seth.'

Seth wheezed with laughter and cracked Robert smartly on the elbow with the head of his cane. 'Well, my lad? Are you buying me that beer, or not?'

Robert's aplomb didn't slip a notch. 'I'd be delighted to, sir.'

'Where did you find the tailor's dummy?' James asked, taking Melody's arm and propelling her back to the ballroom with the dispatch of a drill sergeant on parade.

'Obviously not in the same place as you found your manners,' she replied sharply. 'I'm sorry if you didn't like being coerced into dancing with me yet again, but that's no reason to be so abominably rude.'

He didn't answer for a moment. Instead, he slid his hand down to grasp hers and led her quite gently to the side of the dance-floor. 'It's no excuse at all,' he agreed, 'and I'm sorry. Let's start this conversation over again. You look lovely tonight, Melody, and I would be very honoured if you'd dance with me. Please.'

There were a lot of well-dressed, good-looking men there and Robert was certainly one of them, yet if the word to describe them was handsome, then the word to describe James hadn't yet been invented. Of course he was tall and dashing; of course he had dimples and eye-lashes to kill for. There was no doubt at all that he smiled like an angel, cursed on occasion like the devil, and sometimes indulged in outright bad temper. Heroes always did, didn't they? It was part of their mystique— and also what made them so difficult to domesticate.

Melody looked away. 'The last time we danced, I don't think either of us enjoyed it very much.'

'It will be different this time,' he said, and held open his arms.

The Marilyn Monroe clone who sang with the or-chestra swayed to the microphone and throatily crooned the opening verse of that old smoothie, 'I've Got A Crush On You, Sweetie Pie'. The chandeliers dimmed until they resembled pinpoints of starlight. It was all more than Melody could resist. She went into his arms willingly, settling the crown of her head just below his chin, and let him lead her where he chose, however he chose.

Never mind that half of Port Armstrong society was there to witness the daughter of one of its most revered old families making a spectacle of herself on the dance-floor. Never mind if the way that beautiful body of his moved against hers was little short of indecent. Who gave a fig if he held her so close that they might have been surgically joined from breastbone to thigh? She loved him. It was as simple as that, and she was tired of pretending otherwise.

She knew well enough that a sensible woman didn't fall in love with a set of dimples or a pair of broad shoulders. She looked for other qualities that would endure when the dimples were lost in wrinkles and the shoulders grew stooped with age. If a woman had any brains at all, she traded looks for compatibility and tolerance. She recognised that if a couple couldn't laugh together a woman might spend a lot of time crying—crying for things that had passed her by while she languished over a man who had come into her life one winter and forgotten her by the time summer rolled by.

She knew, too, that, however much he might desire her, James didn't love her back. Sooner or later, the pain of that knowledge would have to be confronted, and then she would hurt and she would cry. But not now. Right now, every instinct she possessed told her to take what little he could offer and treasure it for its brief and lovely duration, because the chance to do so might not pass her way again.

He was worse than certifiable, James decided, folding her a little tighter in his embrace. He was brutal and inhuman to put either her or himself through this. Why in hell hadn't he wriggled off the hook when she'd given him the chance, instead of indulging in such out-right sado-masochism?

As if he didn't know!

He'd been doing so well, until she'd drifted past on the arm of that escort of hers. Then rage had momentarily blinded him and he'd known a primitive urge to grab the poor slob by the throat and roar, 'Get your filthy hands off my woman!'

'His woman', for Pete's sake? Since when?

If he'd harboured any doubt that what he planned to do tomorrow was for the best, that single moment of uncontrolled rage was enough to tell him not only that he'd made the right choice but also that he'd come dangerously close to leaving it too late. Obviously he was living on borrowed time here.

For a man who liked to travel light, he'd picked up a load of excessive baggage in the form of memories that he seemed doomed to carry for the rest of his life.

It was time to tell her. He owed her that much honesty; they'd shared too much for him to justify leaving her to find out from Seth or someone else, like that bitch Chloe. But not quite yet. Just a few minutes more of holding her close like this.

He sighed, and allowed his hand to sneak around her ribcage until the tips of his fingers found the sweet curve of her breast beneath her arm. Lord, but she was lovely in so many ways! Beside the over-dressed, over-adorned women around her, she stood out like a tiny, perfect flower, with bits of her dress hanging down like petals. He would never again smell a rose, heady and sweet after the rain, and not be reminded of her. Ten years from now, he'd be able to close his eyes and recall with perfect clarity the sheen of her hair, the delicate turn of her ankle, the soft, dark depths of her eyes...

'Melody, my dear!' A silver-haired matron bore down on them determinedly. 'Is this *your* young man?'

Melody detached herself a little. 'No.'

'I thought not,' the woman said with evident relief. 'I could have sworn I saw you earlier with that young lawyer, Robert Camberley.' She flashed a meaningless smile at James, and drove home her point. 'Such a gentleman, you understand. Belongs to one of our oldest families.'

Oh, the time had come to cut his losses all right!

'Where are we going?' The music had stopped, but, instead of releasing her, James took her hand firmly in his and steered her towards the lifts at the far side of the foyer.

'To the roof garden,' he said, his tone so sombre that he might have been referring to a morgue.

'James, I can't just disappear without a word to Robert.'

'To hell with Robert!'

She ought to object. Instead, she followed meekly beside him, the warmth she'd found in his arms displaced by the sense of foreboding that had lurked at the back of her mind for days.

From the mansard roof of the old hotel, it was possible to enjoy a three-hundred-and-sixty-degree view of the town and surrounding area. During the summer, the garden terrace was one of Melody's favourite dining spots. She loved sitting at one of the glass-topped tables under a sun umbrella, surrounded by lush tropical plants and hanging baskets overflowing with colourful annuals.

At this time of year, the terrace was closed to the public, but she and James stood in one of the deep window embrasures on the west side of the roof and looked out over the dark waters of the Strait.

'Why have you brought me here, James?' she asked, and wondered if he could hear the edge of fear in her voice.

'I wanted to have a few moments alone with you.'

If only she could take the words at face value! 'Why?'

He heaved a sigh and turned to look at her. He touched her cheek with his fingers, then her mouth. He stroked her hair, then cradled her face as tenderly as if it were made of very rare and very precious porcelain. He touched her as if he were blind, as if he wanted to commit the texture of her to memory.

He felt her tremble and pulled her into the shelter of his arms. She could feel the rapid thud of his heart, the slightly laboured rasp of his breath, and though his hands were warm she continued to shiver, chilled to the bone.

'Melody,' he began hoarsely, 'I...'

Love you? Desire you? She closed her eyes to stem the tears. They were not the words she was going to hear.

'I...' He tried again.

One tear escaped and slid down her face, then another. 'We had a nice dance, this time,' she quavered, frantic to stop him from going on. 'We did, didn't we?'

'Yes,' he said, and pressed her face against his chest. The starched cotton of his shirt blotted up her tears, but nothing could absorb the pain that filled her heart and made her want to die. 'But it was different this time.'

'I don't want to know why.'

'I have to tell you.'

'No,' she begged. 'It was a lovely time we had together. Let's just leave it that.'

'It was the *last* time,' he said relentlessly. 'I'm going away, Melody, back to where I belong.'

'Yes,' she said, swiping at the tears. 'I understand. You have to go to check on things you left behind.'

'I won't be seeing you again.'

'Until the next time...' The words limped past the awful ache in her throat.

'There won't be a next time for us,' he said.

Pride deserted her, along with self-control. 'Don't say that. Please, James, say you don't mean that!'

'I have to go. My life isn't here.'

'But mine is, and I have connections. I could put in a good word...' She stopped and groaned as the realisation of what she was doing sank home.

'You'd like that, wouldn't you?' he replied, distaste curling his beautiful lips. 'Your greatest talent lies in unearthing all a man's vulnerabilities and hanging them out to dry in your back garden for everyone to see.'

Embarrassment stained her cheeks scarlet. 'James, I'm sorry! I didn't mean to insult you.'

'It might interest you to know,' he continued, sweeping aside her apology with the contempt it no doubt deserved, 'that I was offered a job tonight which, in different circumstances, I'd have found hard to turn down. A very prestigious job, Melody, designing reproductions of the old wooden schooners that used to sail out of this harbour back around the turn of the century. There's a growing demand for them, for sea festivals and such, and dear old Port Armstrong is cashing in on the trend with its usual avaricious zeal. In fact the city fathers are so anxious to close a deal with me that I could write my own ticket on how I wanted things done.'

For all his expressed disdain, she could see that he'd been tempted by the challenge of the offer. 'But what an honour for you, James!' she exclaimed, in the faint hope that he'd find her enthusiasm infectious enough to make him reconsider.

'Indeed.' The scorn in his little smile cut her aspirations to ribbons. 'I'm sure your friend who accosted us on the dance-floor would have found it quite acceptable for you to be seen with me, had she known in what high esteem your venerable heritage society holds me.'

'I don't care what my friends think,' she wailed, seeing her hopes crumble into dust. 'I care about you—about us. Why won't you take the job?'

'Because that would mean putting down roots, and I don't belong here. *We* don't belong together.'

'We could, if you'd try.'

'You shouldn't have to try,' he said harshly. 'I've seen too much misery result from people trying to hold on to something that was never meant to work in the first place.'

She looked at him through her tears. I love you, she told him silently.

'Don't,' he said, as though she'd spoken the words aloud. 'I'm not worth it.'

'Isn't that for me to decide?'

'No. You should be looking for someone who shares your background.'

'There's more at stake here than my background. What about us, James?' She drew in a deep, scorching breath and plunged on. 'What about the time we made love? Doesn't that count for anything?'

There, she'd done it, the one thing she'd sworn never to do—assumed the role of woman wronged, and resorted to blackmail. Oh, God, what next?

He didn't flinch. 'We've been playing with fire for weeks, and I blame myself for letting that happen. Now it's up to me to make it stop. Please don't make it any more difficult than it already is.'

He tilted her chin and bent his mouth to hers one last time. Never before had his kiss tasted so sweet or touched her so deeply. When he tore his lips away, he took a part of her heart with him. The pain was excruciating.

He backed away from her until she could no longer feel his warmth. This was how the rest of her life would be, she thought numbly. Empty and cold.

'It's time to say goodbye, my lady,' he said softly. 'Go back to your real life and let me return to mine.'

CHAPTER TEN

ONCE upon a time, Melody would have complied because she wasn't accustomed to having to beg or grovel or make scenes. But that was before James had ignited a passion in her that refused to be hindered either by pride or propriety. At the prospect of losing him, it broke loose with a raging madness that she was helpless to control.

'You *are* my life, James!' she cried, and catapulted herself into his unwilling arms.

She drew in great breaths full of the scent of him. She buried her mouth at the base of his throat and thought she would never forget the flavour of his skin that was not quite aftershave cologne, not exactly spring-water-fresh or winter-cold mountain air, but a blend of all three that was uniquely him.

She didn't understand how she could be so brazen. She couldn't account for where she found the immodest courage or how, tomorrow, she'd manage to look herself in the eye without cringing. All she knew was that whatever drove her to such extremes was highly infectious because, miraculously, James's arms tightened around her and pressed her to him with the same sort of grief-inspired desperation that possessed her.

'Oh, damn,' he muttered into her hair. 'This isn't very ladylike, my darling.'

He was right, and she didn't care, because he could utter all the verbal reproofs he liked and they wouldn't in any way manage to refute the sanction of his body nesting next to hers. Her sexual experience might be limited, but she knew when a man was fighting a losing battle with arousal.

'Right now, I'm just a woman, James,' she half sobbed, twining herself sinuously around him, 'and I need you.'

'No,' he groaned but, at her urging, his hand stole down to the small of her back and inched her closer.

Beguiled, she slid her own hands under his jacket and ran them over his ribs, gauged the tapered strength of his chest, the trim dimensions of his waist, and, at last, dared to flatten possessive palms over his lovely male behind.

'Stop,' he muttered against her mouth, but there was no conviction there, only a simmering heat that threatened to explode. And meanwhile the skirt of her dress inched up over her hips until he found the strip of cool exposed thigh where her silk stockings ended.

'James...' she pleaded, as his fingertip explored the scalloped edge of her panties. 'Oh, please, James...'

And without a thought for the imprudence of such behaviour on the roof terrace of the grand old Ambassador Hotel, she snuggled up against him, rotating her hips connivingly and not caring at all that she was tormenting him beyond the limits of human endurance.

Her whole world narrowed to those stolen extra moments and she would have done anything, anything at all, to stretch them into eternity. 'Make love to me,' she implored, when she really meant, Make me pregnant, because surely, for all that he'd claimed otherwise, he wouldn't walk away from his baby, not after all he'd suffered as a child?

But she'd made a fatal error. As though her words dashed him back to awareness of where he was and why and with whom, he almost flung her from him. 'No,' he said on such a note of finality and with such a look in his eyes that she knew they really had reached the end. 'My God, Melody, how do you expect me to live with myself afterwards?'

She lifted her hands helplessly, then let them fall to her sides. She'd tried everything: reason, persuasion, logic. And when all that failed, she'd fallen back on the oldest trick in the book to try to trap him.

She'd encouraged him to use her body, taken unpardonable liberties with his, preyed on the weakness of his flesh to counteract the unflagging strength of his mind. She'd gambled everything—and ultimately lost because, whether he believed it or not, James was a true gentleman at heart. But her middle name ought to have been Jezebel.

Not unexpectedly, a rehash of the spring ball was the topic under discussion when Melody arrived at the Alley on Monday morning.

'You look pale,' Emile greeted her. 'Are you not yet recovered from dancing till dawn, *ma petite*?'

'"Pale" is putting it mildly. She looks more like the wrath of God,' Chloe amended, eyeing her closely. 'What happened; did lover-boy dump you?'

Melody unlocked the door to Yesteryear before answering. 'Yes.'

For once, Chloe looked embarrassed. 'Oh, well . . . in that case . . .'

'She'll keep her mouth shut,' Roger said, 'before she manages to fit the other foot in it as well.'

'It doesn't matter,' Melody said dully, and it was the truth. She'd lived a lifetime of misery since Saturday night, and shed an ocean of tears, and still the hurt raged. Nothing anyone else said or did could possibly make it any worse. 'I'd as soon have it out in the open and done with. Now you can all say how sorry you are, and what a cad he is, and how lucky I am that I found out before it was too late—whatever that's supposed to mean—and then the nine-week wonder can be put to rest and life can go on as usual.'

Except, of course, that life would never be quite the same again. Nevertheless, she'd have to endure it. People had a habit of surviving heartbreak and humiliation.

Anna Czankowski hurried over with a mug of fresh coffee. 'Please.' She offered a sympathetic smile. 'For you.'

'I hope you gave him hell,' Chloe said.

'Not this child.' Ariadne clucked her tongue disapprovingly. 'She is too soft-hearted. Now I would have made him suffer. He would regret being so foolish much sooner than I would agree to forgive him.'

'I thought the two of you seemed pretty cosy on Saturday night,' Roger said. 'Maybe he'll have a change of heart.'

'I'm sure Roger is right.' Emile nodded agreement. 'You'll see, *ma chère*. Before the day is over, he will be here, with bouquets and apologies.'

'He's left town,' Melody said baldly. 'He won't be back.'

Justin spoke up then. 'How did his father take the news?'

She was ashamed to admit she'd been too preoccupied with her own unhappiness to spare a thought for how Seth was feeling. 'I don't know. I'll stop by after work and find out.'

'Did Logan say why he chose now as the time to go?' Roger asked.

Melody supposed he had, but the memory was blurred. All she knew for sure was that she'd made a fool of herself, begging and pleading with a desperation that might have gone on indefinitely had not James's final rejection induced her bedraggled pride to effect a rescue—of sorts.

Sho'd fled, run away weeping, like the mindless, hysterical heroine in a third-rate melodrama. She hadn't bothered to wait for the lift, but had taken the fire-stairs exit instead. She'd stopped on one of the landings and leaned against the cold iron railing, fighting to catch her breath and control the tears that all but choked her while she straightened her clothing and tried to make herself look semi-decent. Her lungs had felt as if they were on fire.

'I have a headache. Please take me home,' she'd begged Robert, who was too nice to despise a woman for showing such an appalling lack of imagination, and too sensitive to comment on her puffy red eyes.

He'd made their excuses, broken all speed records getting her wrap from the cloakroom and his car from the garage, and had driven her home with no pretence at casual conversation. If he'd noticed the endless stream of tears dribbling down her face, he made no reference to them.

'Thank you,' she'd snuffled when they arrived outside Stonehouse Mansion. 'I'm sorry I can't ask you in for a night-cap.'

'I wouldn't dream of accepting even if you felt you could,' he'd said kindly.

On Sunday morning, a dozen long-stemmed red roses had been delivered to her door. From Robert. May God forgive her, she'd burst out crying all over again because they weren't from James.

'No,' she lied, in answer to Roger's question. 'He didn't say why he had to go now.'

Emile gave her shoulders a squeeze. 'It was a sudden decision, perhaps? A personal emergency?'

'I don't know. I didn't ask.'

'Then you're a fool,' Chloe piped up. 'I'd have made him admit what was so damned important that he had to race away like that on a moment's notice. What do you want to bet he's got a wife and three children waiting for him somewhere? Where *does* he live, by the way?'

'All over the place,' Roger said. 'I got into conversation with his father on Saturday night and he told me. Apparently the guy has an address somewhere on the East Coast, but he spends half his time on site wherever his latest racing yacht is being put through its paces. Last year he was in the South Pacific for four months, and had just come back from six weeks in the Caribbean when he learned about his father's accident. If it's any comfort, Melody, with his sort of wandering lifestyle, it's not likely there's a Mrs Logan waiting in the wings.'

'A man who moves around like that could have several Mrs Logans tucked away,' Chloe observed darkly. 'If you want my opinion, Melody, you're lucky he's out of your life.'

'She doesn't want your opinion,' Ariadne said. 'She wants her beautiful man back, and I can certainly understand why. He was...ah...!' She kissed her fingertips extravagantly. '*Delicious* is the word that comes most readily to mind!'

They meant well, Melody knew, but right at that moment she wished they would all take a running jump into the sea. As for James, the sooner she got him out of her system and decided to fall in love with someone suitable like Robert, the better off she'd be.

Whether or not either man had realised it, both Seth and James had shown subtle signs of a growing fondness for each other. They'd continued to disagree on just about every subject, but their arguments had lost their bite and had become more a matter of enjoyable habit than serious conflict. But even allowing for that, Melody was shocked at the effect James's departure had had on his father.

She found Seth sitting alone in his cottage by the cold ashes in the fireplace, tear tracks drying on his cheek. She felt shamed all over again at her selfish neglect of a man who had virtually lost his only child just when they were getting to know each other and, unlike her, had no other family to turn to for comfort.

'Reckon you know already,' Seth muttered, his weather-beaten old face crumpling. 'The boy's gone and dear only knows when he's likely to be back. Doubt I'll live to see the day. Reckon it'll take having me nailed in my box before he'll set foot in this town again.'

Distressed, Melody knelt beside him and chafed his cold hands in hers. 'He won't wait that long, Seth,' she told him, wishing she believed her own words.

'You know the last time he paid a visit—before this one, that is?' He made a valiant effort to erase the grief by drumming up a dose of resentment. 'Four bloody years! And in between, nothing but a couple of post-cards and a letter every Christmas with a cheque in it—as if money made up for him not being here!'

'You're his father, Seth. He won't forget you.'

'I miss him,' Seth mumbled, groping in his pocket for a handkerchief, 'and the daft part is, I never thought I would. Thought I was past hurting like this.'

'You've still got your friends,' she tried to console him.

He looked at her with a trace of his old spark. 'You still got yours, but that don't stop you missing him, does it? You got your work, and your busy life, too, and you still feel like hell.'

'Pretty soon, Seth, you'll be so involved with the community centre that the days will fly by and you won't have time to miss anyone.'

'T'ain't the days that's the problem, Melody, girl.' He grunted and eased his leg into a more comfortable position. 'No, sir, it ain't the days, it's the nights when a man can't sleep and there ain't anyone to take his mind off all the things he did wrong and never got around to putting right. The nights are the worst.'

Melody nodded, wishing she could disagree. It was possible to dull the pain a little by keeping busy during the days, but the nights were unbearable. 'I know. They're the loneliest times.'

'I'm not just lonely, Melody, I'm alone, and you want to know something?' Seth tried to laugh, but the sound cracked and died before it was properly born. 'I didn't even realise it until the boy came back and made himself at home here. Now this itty-bitty house is so empty-feeling, it rattles. Maybe I should've let him buy me one of them fancy new apartments, like he wanted to. Maybe then I wouldn't keep looking for his face and waiting to hear his voice giving me grief because I don't live my life according the way he thinks I should.'

'But this was never his home, Seth,' she said gently. 'That was the problem, right from the start. Nothing about this town spells home for him.'

Seth sighed. 'I thought,' he said slowly, 'that he might decide he wanted you badly enough to change his mind. I saw how he looked at you sometimes, and that weren't the look of a man who'd got nothing more than an itch that needed scratching—if you'll forgive the expression, which ain't exactly fitting in front of a lady like yourself. But damn it, Melody, girl, I did everything I could think of to bring the pair of you together, and after Saturday night I thought it was working.'

Heaven knew that she'd hoped the same thing herself, on more than one occasion. The first time James had kissed her, the night they'd made love, each had seemed at the time as if it might be the beginning of something wonderful and lasting; and each time she'd learned that, in fact, it had marked a sort of ending. 'I'm afraid things were over long before then, Seth.'

He looked hopeful. 'But you do agree there was something between you?'

'It was a one-sided love-affair, and that kind never works.'

'Reckon it don't at that, and I ought to know, but...' He looked at her searchingly. 'Did you ever tell him you loved him, Melody?'

'No.'

'Maybe you should have. Maybe that would have been enough to make him realise he felt the same way about you.'

'He doesn't trust me enough to love me, Seth, and he refuses to trust himself. Love can't grow in that sort of climate.'

'So I reckon, then, that you won't want to be coming around here any more, being reminded of him and all that.'

'I'll still come to visit. My feelings for James are something separate from my relationship with you.'

She meant every word, but she knew what she had to give wouldn't be enough. Seth needed someone all the time. He needed the comfort of his family, and, although she had to accept that James didn't want her in his life, it angered her to think he could turn his back on his father, too.

March slipped into a cold and blustery April. Squalls raced across the Strait and spat rain against the windows of the Victorian houses, flattening the tulips in the gardens and scattering the blossoms from the flowering cherry trees in soggy drifts along the avenues.

Eventually, Melody started going out again, just to get away from the ongoing misery of her own solitude, but, no matter how busy her schedule, she made a point of stopping by to see Seth every week.

Sadly, each time she saw him it seemed to her that his general state of well-being had deteriorated from the time before. His first question always would be, 'Have you heard from him?' It almost killed her to have to say no, but it was perhaps as well. If she'd known where James could be found, she'd have contacted him and told him exactly what she thought of a man who could establish relationships then sever them without mercy when they threatened to become too demanding. He might like to call it getting on with his life, but in her book it came down to running away, pure and simple. And the person paying the heaviest price for it was his father. She wished she knew how to lessen the pain for him.

And then she found the dog. Late one Friday afternoon, just as yet another soggy day sank into dusk, she was driving along the motorway on the way home from an estate sale in the next town when she noticed the poor old thing practically stagger off the shoulder of the road and under the wheels of the car in front of hers. It never occurred to her not to stop and rescue it. That it hadn't been killed already was nothing short of a miracle.

It was an old and very tired dog with no collar or licence tag to identify it. Its fur was matted, and filthy with gravel and mud, as though it had spent a long time wandering the beaches and highway. Melody doubted it had ever had a bath, let alone been groomed, but she could no more have abandoned it than she could turn her back on Seth.

'How come no one's looking out for you?' she crooned, sliding her arms under the dog's ribs and heaving from behind to get it into the passenger seat of her car. 'You should be home by a fire, not out roaming alone on a night like this.'

'The nights are the worst,' Seth had said. And, 'I'm not just lonely, Melody, I'm alone'.

The words seemed to echo and magnify in her head, telling her plainly enough what her next move should be. If ever a couple had been tailor-made for each other, it was Seth and this dog. Both needed someone to love; both needed to be loved.

'Anyone home?' she sang out, pushing open the front door of the cottage about half an hour later.

Seth limped forward, his face for once creased in its old, familiar grin. But when he saw what she'd brought with her, his expression slid into comic amazement. 'What in Hades you got there, Melody? Talk about something the dog dragged in!'

'I found him—her. She was on the side of the motorway and just about ready to keel over.'

'Reckon I can see that,' Seth said.

'She's a stray, Seth, and needs a home. I can't have a pet in the apartment, but you...' She let the sentence trail off, and took shameless advantage of his soft heart by appealing to him with wide, beseeching eyes.

'Listen, girl, I got something to say...'

It struck her then that he was unusually agitated—distracted, almost—as though there were more pressing problems deserving his attention. 'I couldn't leave her on the motorway, Seth,' Melody countered urgently. 'I might as well have sentenced her to death.'

'I ain't *arguing*,' he said. 'I'm just trying to get a word in edgeways. Thought you ought to know——'

'I stopped and bought some food, and a bowl. And tomorrow I'll get her a collar and a basket, and I'll take her to be groomed,' she went on persuasively, urging the dog towards him. 'And she's smart, I'm sure.'

Obligingly, the poor old thing tottered over and leaned trustingly against Seth's knee. 'Damned thing smells,' he declared, but he bent down and fondled the animal's ears. 'Reckon, since her fur's such a mess, I'll call her Mattie.'

'She needs a bath, I know, but right now she needs a place to sleep even more. Look at her, Seth. She's exhausted.'

'Poor old gal,' Seth agreed, limping to the couch. 'Probably got dumped out of a car because someone decided she weren't worth the trouble of looking after any more, and I reckon I know how that might feel. Come on over here with her so I can sit down and have a closer look. If she's got fleas, Melody, she ain't sleeping on my bed tonight.'

'Then you'll let her stay?'

He glared. 'You knew good and well I'd let her stay, which is why you brought her here in the first place, so don't insult me by pretending to be surprised.'

Melody flung her arms around his neck. 'Oh, Seth, I do love you!'

'You're telling that to the wrong man, girl. And you smell near as bad as that dog! Come to that, your pretty white suit is ruined, you're covered in dirt, and I don't recall ever seeing you look such a mess.'

'You're right.' She ran a hand through her hair. 'Listen, I hate to run off and leave you like this, but I'd better get going. I'm late for a dinner-date as it is.'

'Get on home, then, and leave me and old Mattie to get to know each other.' He offered a wily grin. 'You can come back tomorrow when we feel more like visitors.'

Before she'd closed the door behind her, he was deep in conversation with his dog. She drove home with a rare feeling of satisfaction and realised that she was actually looking forward to the next day. It was a feeling which had been missing from her life for too long.

Port Armstrong's dog-grooming establishments were heavily booked on the weekends. An appointment on a Saturday was, Melody quickly discovered the next morning, quite out of the question unless it was arranged well in advance.

'So,' she announced, showing up at Seth's just after noon, loaded with supplies, 'I came equipped to do the job myself.'

'Before you get started,' Seth said, 'there's something you ought to know, and it can't wait any longer. I wanted to tell you last night but——'

'I think I've got a pretty good idea of what you're going to say.'

His grey eyebrows shot up. 'You do?'

'Yes. I'm taking a lot for granted, saddling you with a dog without even discussing it with you first, and I promise not to make a habit of doing things like that, but I didn't know what else to do. She's too old to survive an animal shelter, and no one would want to adopt her at her age. But I'll help, Seth. I'll take care of her expenses, if you'll give her a home.'

'That ain't what I'm talking about. It's——'

A disturbing through struck her at the rather odd look on his face. 'You haven't changed your mind about keeping her, have you, Seth?'

'No, no, nothing like that. She's a gentle old thing and she'll be company for me.'

'That's how I hoped you'd feel.' Melody sorted through the bag of supplies. 'See, I bought some shampoo and a brush and comb, and there's a plastic baby bath and a basket in my car that I'll get in a minute. Oh, and here's a collar. I hope it'll fit.'

It occurred to her then that the dog was nowhere in sight. 'Where is she, Seth?'

'That's what I was starting to tell you.'

'Oh, lord, don't say she's run away?'

'No.' He laughed. 'Heck, even with this gammy leg I can run faster than she can.'

Melody breathed a sigh of relief. 'Then where is she?'

'Upstairs.'

'*Upstairs*? How in the world did she manage that? She could barely make it into my car last night. And your bedroom's down here, so why would she——?'

'He's back,' Seth said.

Paralysed, Melody stood with one arm still inside the large paper bag. 'What?'

'He's back.' Seth jerked his head towards the stairs.

It was an absurd question, because there was only one possible answer, but she had to ask it anyway. 'Who is?'

Seth's smile blossomed. 'James.'

She felt frozen inside. 'When?'

'This morning. I got a phone call yesterday. That's what I started to tell you last night.' He jerked a thumb at the ceiling. 'He's up there now, unpacking his bag, and the dog went with him.'

'*Why*?'

Seth shrugged. 'Reckon she likes his company.'

'No.' Melody shook her head and tried to quell a wild urge to laugh hysterically. 'Why has he come back, Seth?'

'Says he can't settle down knowing he's got a load of unfinished business to attend to back here. Says he won't take no for an answer about setting me up in style in my old age. Claims he has to get my life in order before he can start on his own.' The familiar grin was laced with delight. 'As if I lived this long without learning to manage by myself!'

Warning bells clanged in Melody's mind, cautioning her not to jump to unwarranted conclusions. Nothing Seth had told her gave her reason to suspect, or hope, that James's return had anything to do with her.

Disappointment set in, thawing the chill and turning her to a seething jumble of emotion from which only one rational thought was able to surface with any clarity.

'I have to get out of here!' she said in a strangled tone.

Quickly, before she made a fool of herself again.

CHAPTER ELEVEN

'OH, NO, you don't!' a voice at Melody's back informed her. 'At least, not before you give this mutt a bath.'

Spinning round, she found James on the bottom stair, the dog bundled under one arm. 'You brought her here, I'm told,' he said, 'so you can clean her up. How are you, Melody?'

She swallowed and tried to drag her eyes away from the sight of him. What a useless effort! He was there, in the flesh, as tall, dark and handsome as ever, and she felt an appalling need to feast her eyes on him indefinitely.

But she'd grovelled enough in front of him and he didn't have to know she was on the verge of doing so again. 'Quite well,' she squeaked.

He smiled, which really undid her. 'What are you hiding in that bag—a gun?'

'No,' she said, adding without thinking, 'I didn't know you'd be here.'

Seth cackled in a way he hadn't cackled in weeks, and even James laughed. 'And here I deluded myself into thinking you might be pleased to see me,' he said, setting Mattie down on the floor.

Melody wasn't about to cave in and admit that her initial reaction had been so overjoyed that she didn't know how she remained earthbound. 'What I meant is that I didn't see your car when I drove up.'

'I don't have one. I took a taxi from the airport.'

She should have guessed it would be, quite literally, a flying visit, but she supposed he deserved a little credit

for showing some sign of conscience where his father
was concerned. 'I'm happy for Seth's sake that you're
here,' she said. 'How long are you planning to stay this
time?'

'I haven't decided.' He glanced at Seth. 'It depends
on a number of things, the first being how long it takes
to make this father of mine see sense.'

'And if you succeed, then what?'

He looked at her so long and steadily that her heart
began to thump unevenly. She waited for him to say
something wonderful, like, Then it's our turn, Melody.
Yours and mine.

Instead, he whistled tunelessly and paced over to the
window. 'Oh . . .' He fiddled with the blind. 'This and
that.'

She glared at his back. 'It sounds critically important,' she snapped, 'so why don't I take the dog
outside and leave you to get on with . . . "this and that"?'

For once, it was sunny, and the cold wind had given
way to a gentler breeze that hinted at summer just around
the corner. The willow tree at the side of Seth's cottage
was in full leaf and a few ancient wallflowers under the
living-room window sent waves of perfume wafting her
way.

Mattie sank down on the warm grass with a grunt of
pleasure and submitted to having the knots combed out
of her fur. 'I wish,' Melody muttered, attacking the job
with energy, 'that you and I could trade places. Your
troubles have come to an end, sweetie, but I have a feeling
mine just started all over again.'

'Talking to yourself is a very bad sign,' a voice at her
back announced, and she realised that James had followed her outside with a pail full of warm water.

'I was talking to the dog,' Melody said.

'Because it's preferable to having to talk to me?'

She dared to look at him. 'Perhaps. You're looking well, James.'

'Which is more than I can say for you.' He strode over and emptied the pail into the plastic bath-tub which she'd brought from the car before she'd started grooming Mattie. 'You're thinner than you should be, Melody,' he observed, squatting down beside her and rolling up the sleeves of his blue cotton shirt. 'Why is that?'

She was tempted to tell him that that was what pining did for a person, that since he'd walked away she'd had no appetite for food and precious little zest for life, but the scent of him was evoking such vivid, intimate memories that she couldn't begin to articulate so lengthy a reply. 'Thin is fashionable,' she croaked instead.

'And it's important to be in fashion.' He picked up the dog and, overcoming her objections, dumped her firmly in the tub and began sluicing water over her hide. 'I'm surprised you'd bother to take on a mutt like this with no pedigree or anything to its name. Why did you bring her to my father? Because Robert wouldn't be seen dead with her?'

She really was a fool to have entertained, even for a moment, the notion that he'd overcome his prejudices and realised that everything he needed and wanted in life was here and included her as well as his father.

Anger rose up at her futile, chronic hope for a miracle from a man who'd made it plain from the beginning that he didn't believe in them. 'This might come as a shock to you, James, but Mattie's lack of bloodlines had nothing to do with my reasons for bringing her to Seth and everything to do with filling his poor, lonely old heart with comfort. And not that it's any of your business, but I haven't seen Robert in weeks.'

Obviously surprised at the vehemence of her reply, James grew very still. 'Does that mean he's out of your life?'

'No. He will always be part of my life. It just happens that he's away on holiday right now.'

'I see. I guess that answers my next question, then.'

'And what question is that?'

James's smile didn't reveal a single dimple. 'That you've realised what a suitable suitor he is, and decided he's worth keeping.'

'James,' she said wearily, 'I collect classic clothes, not suitors. Robert is a friend, and that's all he'll ever be. But just to set the record straight once and for all, when it comes to relationships, whether they're with humans or animals, I look for sensitivity and sincerity, not suitability. I'm no more interested in a man's pedigree than I am in Mattie's. What matters to me is that there's a capacity to love and be loved.' She paused and shook her head. 'But you're such a snob, James, that you probably won't be able to understand any of that.'

'Me, a snob?' He sat back on his heels and laughed incredulously.

'Yes,' she said, massaging shampoo into Mattie's fur. 'From the minute we met, you've refused to see past the obvious. Instead, you've looked down on me, criticised me, and tried to make me feel inferior for the things I can't help, like having been born well-off. You're still doing it, and I've suddenly realised I'm tired of it. It's becoming a bore, James.'

'I came back here to make peace with you,' he bellowed. 'Does that sound like a man who's content only to find fault with a woman?'

'If that's all you want, you might as well go away again. I'm looking for a lot more than that.'

'What else do you want, for crying out loud?'

She shook her head. 'If I have to spell it out for you, then there's no point in discussing it.'

'Well, damn it, Melody, I'm doing my best here. Give me some help.'

'No,' she said, hoping she wouldn't live to regret this last stand at courage. 'I've given you more of myself than I've ever given any other man, and I would have gone on giving as long as I lived. But you were right, James. It's no good if only one person is making the effort, so I'm afraid you'll have to look elsewhere for whatever it is you thought you'd find by coming back here.'

'I came back for you.' He wrenched the bottle of shampoo out of her hand and flung it across the garden. 'Damn it, I came back because I couldn't get you off my mind and because I thought you might be miserable without me.'

'Please spare me your charity,' she said coldly. 'I don't welcome it any more than your father did when I tried to shove it down his throat.'

He let out a string of words never heard in high society. She heard him out, unmoved.

At last he said, 'OK, what do I have to do?'

'Figure it out for yourself,' she told him.

'All right.' He sighed, and looked over his shoulder as if he expected to see a noose hanging from the willow tree. 'Let's get married.'

Her heart almost skidded to a halt, but she managed to hang on to a semblance of composure. 'No, thank you,' she said politely.

'Why not?'

'Figure that out for yourself, too.'

'You're trying my patience, woman!'

He was breaking her heart. Again. 'How inconsiderate of me.'

'You know, Melody,' he said, swiping away a blot of shampoo that had floated up and attached itself to his shirt front, 'sarcasm ill becomes you. You know what I'm trying to say. Why is it so important that I find exactly the right words?'

'Because I won't believe you mean them unless you can bring yourself to say them.'

He cursed again. 'I'm here, aren't I?'

'It's not enough, James.' She scooped a handful of loose dog hair coated with soap scum from the surface of the water, then grasped the edge of the bath-tub and started to lift it.

'What do you think you're going to do with that?'

'I ought to crown you with it, but instead I'm going to empty it, then fill it with clean water so that I can rinse off the dog. Then I'm going home.'

'Damn it, give the thing to me! What are you trying to prove—that I'm such a boor I'd let a woman struggle with something that weighs almost as much as she does?'

'No. That I'm not afraid to get my hands dirty by taking on whatever chore needs to be done.'

He stopped raving long enough to look her over. 'Not just your hands,' he remarked. 'You've got a streak of mud across your face and those clothes you're wearing will never be the same again.' A reluctant grin softened his expression. 'Aren't you a bit too old to be playing in the dirt, my lady?'

'I don't care.'

'I do,' he said softly, and reached out to touch her.

She shied away. 'Please don't.'

'Why not, Melody?'

'Because,' she said unsteadily, 'I don't trust you.'

He looked away. 'I was afraid you might not. Tell me how to change that, Melody.'

He didn't know how tempted she was, but she'd come too far to back down now. She couldn't give him any more answers. He had to want them badly enough to find them out for himself.

Mattie chose that moment to remind them that she was still only half bathed by shaking and showering them both with dirty water and loose dog hair.

James seized on the diversion with alacrity. 'Oh, great! Now we're even wetter than she is.' He grimaced and dried off his face with his hands. 'Go on home and change into some dry clothes, Melody, and leave me to finish up here.'

Not, 'I'll call you later,' or 'Can we get together and finish this conversation another time?' In fact, the way he latched on to the first excuse that presented itself to change the subject was enough to make her wonder exactly how sincere he'd been in the first place about wanting to repair the damage to their relationship.

Her doubts multiplied when the rest of the weekend and half the next week passed without another word from him. And then, on Thursday morning, just before the Alley opened for business, two dozen pale pink roses were delivered to the boutique, and this time they were from James.

Their arrival caused quite a flurry of excitement. Within seconds her neighbours had abandoned their own shops and crowded into hers.

'Who are they from?' Ariadne wanted to know.

'James Logan,' Roger said, reading the card over Melody's shoulder. 'And he wants to have dinner with her on Saturday night.'

Chloe shook her head in disgust. 'I suppose you're going to accept?'

'Of course she is, you foolish woman,' Ariadne replied scornfully.

'In that case,' Chloe told Melody, with the nearest thing to affection she'd ever shown, 'you'd better come into my shop during your lunch break and take a look at the latest shipment of French lingerie. If you're going to make a fool of yourself again, you might as well do it in style.'

'And I have a pair of antique earrings that you may borrow for the occasion,' Emile said.

'I would offer a Russian sable, but the weather has grown so warm,' Ariadne mourned, then brightened as an idea struck. 'Of course, if all you had on underneath was Chloe's French lingerie——'

'Ariadne!' Emile scolded.

'Just don't let him walk all over you,' Roger advised.

'Remember,' Ariadne said, 'make him suffer a little.'

Anna Czankowski murmured something unintelligible. 'It's an old Polish proverb wishing for luck in love,' Frederic explained. 'We hope for much happiness for you this time, Melody.'

'It's only a dinner-date,' Melody protested.

'I think it is more,' Emile said. 'A man does not come all the way across the country just to take a woman out to dinner.'

She couldn't help but be warmed by their concern and excitement. For all the squabbling and disagreeing that took place among them, they seemed to care about what happened to her. The most touching indication came from Chloe, who plopped a ribbon-tied box on Melody's glass counter just before the Alley closed on Friday night.

'I didn't get around to giving you this before Christmas,' she said offhandedly, which was a blatant lie since they never exchanged Christmas gifts. 'Sorry it's a bit late.'

Melody lifted the lid and gasped with pleasure. 'This is the most exquisite underwear I've ever seen. Thank you, Chloe!'

Chloe shrugged. 'Pink seems to be your colour, and I'm never going to be able to sell that particular set—it's too small—so enjoy.'

Melody hoped she'd be able to do just that, but she was nervous, so nervous that she changed her outfit three times before James rang her bell at seven-thirty on Saturday night and, if he'd arrived ten minutes later, she'd probably have changed it again. What, after all, did a woman wear when her whole future lay on the line? Because there was little doubt about it: tonight, she and James either made a go of things, or went their separate ways forever.

Of course, he looked absolutely beautiful, in a strong, masculine way, wearing a black pin-striped suit, white shirt and silver-grey tie, all of it doing marvellous things for his tanned skin and blue eyes. He also looked very formal, and she was glad she'd finally settled on a peach crêpe dinner dress, cut along the lines of a late-Victorian tea gown and trimmed extravagantly with gold lace. If nothing else, they made a well-dressed couple.

He'd made reservations at L'Auberge Royale, a very fine restaurant in what had been the home of a French count back at the turn of the century. The dining-room looked out on formal gardens approaching early summer perfection. Huge magnolias and lilacs in full bloom perfumed the soft air. Lilies of the valley filled tiny crystal vases on the linen-draped tables, candles glimmered in the dusk, and, as if all that didn't spell romance enough, a violinist wandered about the room, seducing guests with haunting tunes about love.

'You're probably wondering,' James observed as they sipped wine between the appetiser and the main course, 'why I waited almost a week before getting in touch after our last conversation.'

'I stopped trying to second-guess you a long time ago, James,' Melody said.

'I had a lot of business to attend to, and I wanted it all over and done with before I saw you again.'

'Does that mean you've tied up all those loose ends that brought you back here?'

He nodded. 'More or less. I managed to convince my father to move to something more comfortable. I bought him another house.'

The little bubble of optimism that had somehow slipped past the barriers of caution she'd erected died an early death. So he'd been toying with her emotions again, after all. It was filial concern that had brought James back to town, and nothing more. 'How kind.'

'Too little and almost too late is more like it.' He slanted a glance at her from under lowered brows. 'You probably think I'm the worst kind of son, and you're probably right. Family and such has never meant that much to me until recently, but it's always been important to you, hasn't it?'

'Yes,' she said, and stared glumly at the glazed lamb tenderloin the waiter slid before her.

'Have you ever wondered,' James went on conversationally, 'how you'd react if your family disowned you because they didn't approve of the man you married?'

'That would never happen.'

'It might,' he said, nodding to the waiter to bring a second bottle of wine. 'I've seen it happen a dozen times, especially when money enters the picture. Fathers don't like to think their daughters are falling victim to fortune-hunters.' He picked up his glass, then set it down again. 'So what would you do if your family didn't approve of your choice, Melody?'

'I'd trust my heart,' she said, 'and I'd trust my family to accept my choice, because I know the thing that matters most to them is that I'm happy.'

'Even if they thought the man you chose wasn't really good enough for you?'

'What matters is that *I* think he's good enough for me, and that he thinks I'm good enough for *him*. I believe some people call that love, James.'

He ran his fingertip over the rim of his glass. 'I have a confession to make,' he said, smiling sheepishly. 'Until recently, I had this crazy notion that falling in love was a bit like the common cold: something I could control if I took the proper precautionary measures.'

'How romantic,' she said faintly.

'I'm inclined to be opinionated and stubborn, and disposed to reaching hasty and sometimes ill-conceived conclusions about things I don't necessarily know very much about.'

'I've noticed.'

'You're looking very solemn. Don't you care for your lamb?'

You're giving me indigestion! she felt like screaming. Where's this conversation leading us? 'It's delicious.'

'Then hurry up and finish. I want to show you something in the garden.'

The trees outside were strung with hundreds of miniature lights that turned the night into a fairyland. James took her elbow and led her away from the restaurant and over the lawns to a tall cedar hedge growing along the far end of the spacious grounds.

'Take a look through here,' he directed, stopping before a small gap in the branches, 'and tell me what you see.'

Vividly conscious of him standing close behind, she obeyed. Then she almost forgot about him at the sight that met her eyes. 'It's a house,' she whispered, her breath catching.

He placed a hand on her hip to steady her and rested his chin lightly on her head. 'Very good, Melody. Now tell me what you think of it.'

The grand old mansion sat surrounded by manicured gardens on what must have been an acre of land. Its windows glowed bronze from the dying rays of the sun. Tall, graceful chimney-pots poked up into the deepening twilight. Mellow brick flowed around cornices and over balcony walls. 'I think it's the most beautiful place I've ever seen!'

'That's the house I bought for Seth,' James said.

'For Seth?' The spiked heels of her gold sandals sank into the grass as she swivelled round to face him. 'James, the place is huge! Whatever possessed you?'

'Oh, not that one,' he said dismissively. 'The gate-house beyond the rhododendron bush.'

'I can't see over the rhododendron bush, James. What gatehouse?'

His hands slipped to her waist. 'I forgot you're not very tall,' he said. 'Let me give you a boost.'

She was entirely too forgettable as far as he was concerned! 'The last time you did this,' she felt constrained to remind him as he shot her four feet into the air, 'I wound up falling on my face.'

'Ah, but I've got a much firmer grip this time,' he murmured, settling her on his shoulder. 'Now, what do you think of Seth's house?'

'It's darling,' she said, squinting a little to make out the gingerbread fretwork around the eaves of the smaller structure half hidden behind the shrubbery. 'It's perfect. But what are you going to do with the other one? Start an orphanage?'

'Something like that,' he agreed, and, before she had time to register dismay or disappointment or any of the other sentiments that seemed to make up the inventory of her emotions where James was concerned, he grasped her by the hips and lowered her slowly to the ground, an inch at a time.

'Now that,' he murmured, when her toes at last made contact with the lawn, 'was a mistake. It's given me the most ungentlemanly urge to kiss you, and I've tried so hard tonight to be the perfect gentleman.'

'Stop trying, and follow your natural instincts instead,' she begged, giving up a battle she'd never had a hope of winning, and swaying towards him. 'I'm tired of waiting.'

He gave her a little shake. 'Let's not repeat past mistakes,' he chided, and marched her firmly back to the dining-room.

During their absence, the waiter had cleared away the remains of the main course and left little silk-tasselled dessert menus propped up in their place. A candle burned in a heavy crystal holder, and to one side a bottle of champagne chilled in a silver ice bucket.

'So,' James said briskly. 'What do you fancy for dessert?'

'Nothing,' Melody said. The truth was that she felt sick from the emotional see-saw of the last two hours and more than a little humiliated at having begged once again for his favours.

'Pity,' James said. 'Humour me, then, and help me pick something out. I've got a craving for something sweet to finish off the evening.'

'You don't need my help in making decisions,' she said.

He lowered his menu and looked at her solemnly. 'In this case, I do, Melody. Please, help me make a choice.'

Listlessly, she flipped open the folded parchment and pretended to scan the page. 'Fresh strawberries,' she said, without bothering to read what was actually offered.

'I don't see them mentioned.'

'Good French restaurants always serve fresh strawberries, James.'

'Not this one,' he persisted. 'It appears to offer something quite different. Take another look.'

For the sake of peace, she complied. Then she had to read the menu twice, because the first time she mistakenly thought that there was a dessert named Melody. 'Oh, for heaven's sake!' she gasped, finally taking in the words squeezed halfway down the page between the rest of the handwritten lines.

Melody, will you be my lady?

'James,' she began, wanting to believe what she saw and afraid to do so, 'this isn't exactly a dessert menu. It's a...a...'

'Marriage proposal,' he supplied.

She felt breathless, spellbound, star-struck! 'But how did it get in here?'

'I bribed the *maître d'*.'

'James, how romantic!'

'That's how I hoped you'd feel.'

She blinked, still unable to believe her eyes. 'No one's ever done anything like this for me before.'

'I should hope not,' he said.

She smiled at him, the candlelight blurring in her eyes. 'I don't know what to say.'

'"Yes" would do for a start.'

She saw then that he was not quite as in charge of the moment as he'd like her to believe. The self-confidence had slipped to reveal a terrible uncertainty. But she had her own insecurities to lay to rest. 'There's something missing, James.'

'Yes. I've known for quite a long time that my life was incomplete, that I needed something more. *Someone*. My mistake lay in thinking it was up to me to decide whether or not I could afford to let that someone be you.' He reached over and took her hand. 'I'm sorry it took me so long to learn differently.'

They were comforting words, wonderful words, but they weren't the words she had to hear. 'That's not exactly what I was talking about.'

'I know. I haven't told you that I love you. It seemed to me, after everything I've put you through, that that was something I had to be brave enough to do in person.'

He kissed her fingers one at a time. 'I didn't choose love, Melody, it chose me. It chose you. And for me to deny that is as pointless as denying that Seth is my father and I'm his son.'

He fished in his pocket then and produced a black velvet jeweller's box. Snapping open the lid, he lifted out a beautiful antique ring.

'These aren't the biggest diamonds in the world, my lady,' he said, 'nor even the most expensive, but they're the best I can afford right now.'

'Oh, James!' Her eyes swam with tears. 'Don't you know yet that your best will always be good enough for me?'

He slid the ring on her finger. It fitted perfectly. 'Will you mind having your father-in-law live next door?'

'No,' she said, and looked at him searchingly. 'You've made a lot of drastic changes, James, and arrived at some far-reaching conclusions.'

'Yes,' he said, 'and I want you to know that I've done so willingly. I love you, Melody. I'm not sure I deserve you, but I do love you and I want to marry you.'

'Are you sure?'

'Very sure.' He fixed her with those bright blue eyes that had taken on a smoky lavender haze, and let her see the evidence for herself without making any attempt to hide it. 'One of the reasons I've always loved the sea and ships is that they represented an escape for me, a promise of something better over the horizon than what I found at home. But I don't need to escape any longer. I've found what I was looking for right here where I started out.'

'What about your work?'

'I can design racing yachts anywhere. And just for a change of pace, I've decided to take the city fathers up on their offer to design reproductions of those early sailing-ships. I'm putting down roots and making a place for myself here, where both our families belong.' He smiled, and she melted. 'Any more questions?'

'No.' She turned her hand over in his and held him tightly. 'You've just answered every one that ever mattered. I would be proud and honoured to marry you.'

' "Proud and honoured" are very fine words, and just the sort I'd expect from you, my lady,' he growled, standing up so abruptly that his chair fell over. 'But you're stuck with a man who doesn't always remember to behave like a gentleman, so I hope you won't mind too much if I kiss you in front of all these nice people who are so busy listening in and watching our every move.'

'I'd be proud and honoured all over again,' she said.

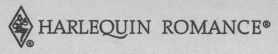
HARLEQUIN ROMANCE®

brings you

More Romances Celebrating Love, Families and Children!

Next month, look out for Emma Goldrick's new book,
Leonie's Luck, Harlequin Romance #3351
(a heart-warming story of romantic involvement between
Leonie Marshal and Charlie Wheeler, who marches
without warning—or permission—into her life!)

Charlie's nine-year-old daughter, Cecilia, who comes to
live with them—at Leonie's Aunt Agnes's invitation—is
somehow never far from what is going on and plays an
innocent part in bringing them together!

Available wherever Harlequin books are sold.

Fifty red-blooded, white-hot, true-blue hunks
from every State in the Union!

Look for MEN MADE IN AMERICA! Written by some
of our most popular authors, these stories feature some
of the strongest, sexiest men, each from a different state
in the union!

Two titles available every month at your favorite
retail outlet.

In February, look for:
THE SECURITY MAN by Dixie Browning
(North Carolina)
A CLASS ACT by Kathleen Eagle (North Dakota)

In March, look for:
TOO NEAR THE FIRE by Lindsay McKenna (Ohio)
A TIME AND A SEASON by Curtiss Ann Matlock
(Oklahoma)

You won't be able to resist MEN MADE IN AMERICA!

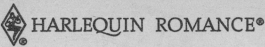

HARLEQUIN ROMANCE®

Last month we announced our Sealed with a Kiss series, which starts in March. This is just to tell you about our choice for that month which we know you will love!

Invitation to Love is the story of Heidi who needs to make a living for herself, but when that livelihood involves welcoming into her home handsome Dillon Archer—the man she believes caused her father's death—she's forced to swallow her pride!

Don't miss Harlequin Romance #3352
Invitation to Love
by Leigh Michaels

Available in March, wherever Harlequin books are sold.

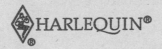

HARLEQUIN®

Don't miss these Harlequin favorites by some of our most distinguished authors!
And now, you can receive a discount by ordering two or more titles!

HT#25577	WILD LIKE THE WIND by Janice Kaiser	$2.99	☐
HT#25589	THE RETURN OF CAINE O'HALLORAN by JoAnn Ross	$2.99	☐
HP#11626	THE SEDUCTION STAKES by Lindsay Armstrong	$2.99	☐
HP#11647	GIVE A MAN A BAD NAME by Roberta Leigh	$2.99	☐
HR#03293	THE MAN WHO CAME FOR CHRISTMAS by Bethany Campbell	$2.89	☐
HR#03308	RELATIVE VALUES by Jessica Steele	$2.89	☐
SR#70589	CANDY KISSES by Muriel Jensen	$3.50	☐
SR#70598	WEDDING INVITATION by Marisa Carroll	$3.50 U.S. $3.99 CAN.	☐ ☐
HI#22230	CACHE POOR by Margaret St. George	$2.99	☐
HAR#16515	NO ROOM AT THE INN by Linda Randall Wisdom	$3.50	☐
HAR#16520	THE ADVENTURESS by M.J. Rodgers	$3.50	☐
HS#28795	PIECES OF SKY by Marianne Willman	$3.99	☐
HS#28824	A WARRIOR'S WAY by Margaret Moore	$3.99 U.S. $4.50 CAN.	☐ ☐

(limited quantities available on certain titles)

	AMOUNT	$
DEDUCT:	**10% DISCOUNT FOR 2+ BOOKS**	$
ADD:	**POSTAGE & HANDLING** ($1.00 for one book, 50¢ for each additional)	$
	APPLICABLE TAXES*	$_____
	TOTAL PAYABLE (check or money order—please do not send cash)	$_____

To order, complete this form and send it, along with a check or money order for the total above, payable to Harlequin Books, to: **In the U.S.:** 3010 Walden Avenue, P.O. Box 9047, Buffalo, NY 14269-9047; **In Canada:** P.O. Box 613, Fort Erie, Ontario, L2A 5X3.

Name:_____

Address: _____ City:_____

State/Prov.:_____ Zip/Postal Code:_____

*New York residents remit applicable sales taxes.
 Canadian residents remit applicable GST and provincial taxes.

HBACK-JM2